When the Guns Were Turned On Us
North American Empire
Series #1

Christopher McGarry

Published by Chris McGarry

Facebook: Sign up for Chris McGarry's mailing list at
https://www.facebook.com/chrismcgarry36/

Follow on Twitter: @ChrisMcGarry2
Pinterest: https://www.pinterest.com/atlantica_79/

Preface

The unthinkable nightmarish scenario conspiracy theorists had presaged for decades-one in which the vast majority of the population of North America largely dismissed as the rantings of paranoid right-wingers-had finally come to fruition. Roughly two years had passed since the once-unstoppable United States of America experienced a catastrophic event economists had been predicting for over a decade-the collapse of the once-mighty American greenback. The period succeeding the 2008 Financial Crash had slowly plunged the U.S., Canada along with every western nation into turmoil and triggered a third world conflict of near biblical proportions.

A year had passed since the United States, NATO and Israel had declared war on the newly-formed alliance of nations comprised of the Russian Federation, China, Iran, Malaysia, Indonesia, Pakistan, Brazil, as well as the Islamic States of the Middle East and Central Asia. The majority of American and Canadian forces had been deployed in the main theatres of Syria, Korea, Iran, Iraq and Ukraine to fight alongside their NATO allies in addition to troops from Australia and New Zealand.

The United States had descended into complete anarchy following the collapse of the economy, an event that greatly affected the economies of neighboring Canada and Mexico. Daily food riots were a common occurrence. After nearly fifty years of a porous border between the U.S. and Mexico, the southern half of the country was flooded with millions of refugees as well as violent street gangs from Mexico, Guatemala, El Salvador and Honduras.

Canada was ruled by a Liberal/New Democrat/Green coalition. The country's oil and gas industries had been ravaged by the global economic meltdown. Desperate to preserve what was left of their economies, the leaders of Canada, the U.S., Mexico, all of Central America together with each Caribbean nation reached an agreement to form a political union and adopt a common currency, the Amero.

Denver, Colorado, had been selected as the capital of this vast new world republic. Maximillian Asher, a long-serving, charismatic yet notoriously sociopathic-minded Republican senator, was handpicked to be president for life by the cabal of international bankers and elites who now had complete dominion over the entire continent.

The extreme right-wing former senator from Georgia used the mass civil unrest and lawlessness brewing throughout much of his empire to clamp down on all disobedience. The Constitution and Bill of Rights, the Canadian Charter of Rights and Freedoms plus the constitutions of each and every nation merged into North America were deemed null and void. Asher declared martial law. Hundreds and thousands of United Nations troops, under the guise of maintaining order, were brought in to the major cities of North America to quell dissent and terrorize the populace.

Across North America, as many as two million libertarian activists, environmentalists, gun owners, Christians-anyone that actively opposed or was considered a threat to the regime-were rounded up and placed into "re-education" centres, most of which were either former correctional institutions or facilities set up on military bases.

The merger of the former nations of North America also brought all levels of law enforcement under one banner. Every agency ranging from small town sheriff's departments, state and provincial police forces to the RCMP, Department of Homeland Security and the Mexican Federal Police were all unified under the federal North American Police.

Most large counties in Canadian provinces and American states were placed under the governorship of administrators, high-ranking bureaucrats appointed by President Asher himself. In British Columbia, all electoral districts were ruled by these administrators.

Chapter 1

The various dire issues affecting the world were the furthest thing from Jake Scribner's mind on this warm late-April morning. Crusty sleep still embedded into the corners of his hazelnut brown eyes, Jake sauntered into the living room of the two-storey home he'd purchased nearly a year earlier in the Kamloops suburb of Batchelor Hill. Glorious rays of sunshine penetrated through the east-facing windows of the house. Jake had recently turned forty. At an age when many men put on what is commonly referred to as 'middle-age spread', Jake maintained a lean, borderline ripped figure.

Hanging from the walls of the living room were reminders of both his distant and recent pasts. They included portraits of Jake, his sister, Samantha, and their parents including one taken five years earlier of him outfitted smartly in his crisp United States Air Force Uniform, the hard-earned scarlet beret of a combat controller atop his head. Jake was the oldest child of an American father and Canadian mother who had divorced when he was just eight years old. Jake and Samantha had spent their childhoods living between Hamilton, Ontario, and San Diego, California. Shortly after graduating from high school in San Diego, as a dual citizen he was eligible to enlist in the United States Air Force. He had retired a year earlier with the rank of master sergeant.

Jake flicked on the coffee maker. Nicole Clare, the fun-loving country girl he had met not long after settling down in Kamloops, had already put water and ground coffee in the filter the night before. Nicole and her seven-year-old daughter, Arielle, were still asleep upstairs.

Jake took out a hard plastic cutting board. He took tomatoes, red, yellow and green peppers from the fridge and cut them up into little pieces along with onions and cheese. This was for the omelets he was preparing to make for the three of them. As a youth, Jake had spent some time in the interior of British Columbia. He was enthralled by the sheer beauty of the region; the mountains, shimmering blue lakes, pockets of arid desert, vineyards and the expansive reaches of Lac Des Bois Provincial Park, a stone's throw away from his front doorstep. After he had finished cutting up the veggies, Jake took out a carton of eggs.

*****

It had been the first night Nicole Clare had taken off in close to a month. Her body and mind still tired, she struggled to pull herself out of bed. In addition to her job as a researcher for Analytic Chemicals, the pleasant-faced, petite but strong thirty-three-year-old single mother operated a blog that saw upwards of two-hundred thousand visitors each day. Nicole was the daughter of Francine and Bill Clare, who operated one of the largest ranches in the Thompson-Nicola region. Renowned for her sharp wit and literary talent, Nicole wasn't afraid to make her views known about hot-button issues such as big government, censorship, abortion, gun rights or the American takeover of Canada.

Nicole went downstairs. Jake and Arielle were seated at the kitchen table slowly eating their veggie omelets. She made a beeline for the coffeemaker. She took down a mug from the cupboard and poured. The strong Colombian roast revitalized her drowsy senses. Nicole sat down at the table.

"You look like somebody who is well-rested," Nicole said to her fiancé as she took a sip of her coffee.

For the down-to-earth small town B.C. girl, meeting the ruggedly-built former Special Operations soldier was classic love at first sight. Nicole adored Jake's outgoing, funny personality and his eagerness to always want to do something fun. Like Jake, Nicole, when time permitted, enjoyed various outdoor pursuits such as camping, swimming, hiking and even target shooting. Jake, who had remained a bachelor up to this point, was looking forward to spending the rest of his life with Nicole. They had already discussed the possibility of her having another child.

"I've been getting up early most mornings since I was eighteen," Jake stated. "So, what do you ladies have planned for today?"

"Well, we have to get the house cleaned for tomorrow. My parents as well as my uncle Frank are coming over for dinner. That's at five by the way," Nicole explained.

"I'll be there. Don't you worry," Jake said with a smile.

Jake was alerted by the sound of an armored military vehicle driving down Benton Street. He arose from the table and peered out the kitchen window. A North American Police armored personnel carrier moved slowly down the suburban street. It was one of countless former military vehicles that had been 'donated' to law enforcement agencies throughout the continent.

"A bunch of those jackbooted thugs again?" Nicole asked with disdain in her voice.

"Yes." Jake sat back down. As of yet, there had not been many signs of the crackdown on freedoms the republic was currently under. Other than the odd NAP patrol, the region was relatively quiet.

Nicole sipped the remainder of her coffee. A few days earlier, she had caught wind of a popular civil liberties activist from Victoria who'd allegedly been detained along with dozens of others.

"Jake, you know how I feel."

Jake could sense the fear and trepidation in the tone of her voice. In his mind, the entire world had gone completely insane. And he was trying to make sense of it all. Like most citizens, the former airman simply wanted to be left alone to live his life.

"I spoke to somebody a couple of days ago who told me that I need to be extremely cautious about expressing my views. I'm getting scared Jake. I don't mean to get paranoid in front of you and my daughter but this whole situation is getting really frightening. I just have a feeling something catastrophic is coming down the pipe."

Jake put his arm around Nicole's shoulders.

"You're not the only one who feels that way. How do you think I feel? I didn't spend twenty years risking life and limb just so our beautiful countries could be transformed into the Fourth Reich. I promise both of you. Should anything bad happen, I will be there to protect both of you. And I always make good on my promises," Jake exclaimed adamantly.

Chapter 2

It certainly wasn't the most glamorous assignment Frank Carragher had ever been given by his superiors. Nothing like the postings he'd had in Montreal, Ottawa, Washington, D.C. or even Canberra, Australia, when he had worked with the Canadian embassy. The eldest of three children who were raised in the affluent

Montreal suburb of Westmount, Carragher had known nothing but privilege for all of his fifty-five years. Not that his childhood had been a shining success. While growing up, the considerably overweight man had lacked the ability of many of his peers to excel in sports. His often overbearing father, a bank manager, had expected too much of the awkward young man, constantly putting him down. He had earned a degree in business administration from McGill University and from there began a long career with the public service of Canada.

Over a span of thirty years, Carragher had fought and schemed his way up the fiercely competitive bureaucratic ladder, holding a variety of high management positions in various departments and agencies. A close-cropped beard covered a hammy, slightly-wrinkled face. The senior bureaucrat had an austere mien; it was next to impossible to force a smile. To compensate for his self-confidence that had been shattered, as a youth, Carragher had developed an unhealthy obsession with gaining power. He craved power and monopoly over others the way a junkie craves his next fix.

At the time of the merger, Carragher had been working with the Department of Justice. At first, he was a bit hesitant to leave Ottawa and the comforts of his million-dollar home for some nondescript city in the interior of British Columbia.

It quickly dawned on his bitter, scheming mind that the Thompson-Nicola district could become his own little fiefdom. It was simply too good of an opportunity to pass up. The seat of administrative power for the district was the Jim Canfield Building located in the heart of downtown Kamloops. Its prior status had been the home of several B.C. Provincial Government regional offices. There was a knock at the office door.

"Come in." Carragher said flatly.

Carli, a young, somewhat naïve woman peeked inside.

"Mr. Carragher, Major Toombs is here."

"Send him in."

Though they shared similar views, Major Dan Toombs and Frank Carragher came from very different backgrounds. The six-foot-one, two-hundred pound Toombs had been raised in a strict fundamentalist Baptist family in Birmingham, Alabama. Fiercely patriotic almost to the point of being blinded, Toombs eagerly wanted to serve his country. He had received a scholarship to West Point. With his shifty eyes and close-cropped black moustache, Toombs appeared dashing, though in a villainous way. He'd spent twenty years in the United States Army, twelve of them as a ranger. When the North American Police was formed, he was hired on and permitted to keep his rank from the U.S. Army.

Toombs entered, dressed in the jet-black long-sleeved buttoned shirt and pants commonly worn by commissioned officers in the NAP. Carragher rose from his desk.

"Welcome major." Carragher extended his hand as he greeted the career soldier.

The men shook hands.

"You're certainly a long way from home."

"I certainly had my misconceptions about Canada," Toombs stated in a slow Southern drawl. "It's actually quite okay up here."

"I was to the Yellowhammer State once. Passed through on my way to New Orleans. Anyway, we should start discussing how we are going to govern his district."

"Sir, I must say that I'm a tad peeved that the NAP's northwestern division is only giving me three-hundred and fifty personnel." Carragher could tell his subordinate was angry." For crying out loud! This district is over forty-five thousand miles, sorry, kilometers. I really don't know what in the name of God is going through the minds of those pencil pushers in Seattle. I require more personnel if I am to maintain order."

"You have to admit, it was a rather intelligent move on their part," Carragher stated. "Fly those NAP troopers in on commercial airliners as not to spook the generally dumbed-down populace. In addition to the twenty APCs, there are two surveillance helicopters. We are also getting a contingent of UN…"

"About them, what is their country of origin?"

"The United Kingdom. British Parachute Regiment," Carragher replied. "Their role will be to guard the bridges that cross the North and South Thompson Rivers and the airport, as well as vital pieces of infrastructure, including that massive substation on the outskirts of the city. They are on their way here now."

Toombs mulled this over.

"Paras." He nodded his head with approval. "Tough outfit for sure."

"To further assist us in quelling any resistance that may arise, the Brits are keeping a squadron of Apache attack helicopters at the airport," Carragher explained.

"Sir, I'm afraid that if we don't clamp down hard on even the slightest show of insubordination, resistance will be a real possibility. Just look at northern Washington State, right along the border. Rebelliousness spreads like wildfire. I'm just thankful that your government, well, what used to be the Canadian government, had the good sense to abolish the private ownership of firearms."

"Major Toombs, I can see that you indeed have many misconceptions about Canada that have been engrained into the American psyche. Some frozen, pussified, socialist paradise. In fact, truth be told, there is a higher rate of gun ownership in the Great White North than in the Land of the Free and Home of the Brave. Take into account that we are in western Canada. Very conservative and libertarian-minded. One would have to be incredibly naïve to actually believe that every citizen dutifully handed in their weapons to authorities. Mark my words, there are hundreds and thousands of guns buried in the ground all over B.C., Alberta, Saskatchewan…indeed, the entire country. And people are merely waiting for the right time to dig them up."

"Sir, the list. May I see it?"

"I nearly forgot about that."

Carragher retrieved a sheet of paper from a desk drawer. He handed it to Toombs.

"As with every city, Kamloops has its share of citizens who hold subversive views and are liable to cause trouble," Carragher said.

Toombs looked over the list.

"These are two hundred names and addresses my staff has compiled," Carragher explained. "Some are libertarians; others belong to gun rights or free speech organizations. Being as this is B.C, there are a handful of environmental radicals on there as well."

"Sir, what truly concerns me is the ex-military people, those with the skills to construct weapons and train fellow citizens to fight as insurgents. It is imperative to keep a lid on them," Toombs said with urgency in his voice.

"We will be doing our best to keep a lid on everybody." Carragher looked out of the expansive window of his office into the city below. On the flagpole in front of the Jim Canfield Building where the Canadian flag once flew proudly, the new flag of North American stood in its place. The design was an unusual melding of the colors of the Mexican and U.S. flags with a red maple leaf in front of them.

"Major, once all of those individuals have been arrested, some will be housed in the former regional correctional centre on the outskirts of the city while others are being shipped to labor camps in the mountains."

Chapter 3

The backs of fifty-five members of the British Parachute Regiment vibrated as they sat against the walls of the payload area of the Chinook CH2 helicopter as it flew over the border between Canada and the United States. The men, ranging in age from early twenties to forty, wore multi-terrain pattern camouflaged combat fatigues. Their gear was nestled on the floor around them. Half an hour earlier, a contingent of the British Armed Forces personnel and vehicles flying on two Chinook helicopters and two massive Hercules transport planes had left Fairchild Air Force Base in Washington State. Their destination: Kamloops Regional Airport, now completely under the control of the Federal Government.

Lieutenant-Colonel Allister Mullen sat pensively on either side of his staff, Lieutenant Raymond Brown and Captain Sean Wynne. Brown was dozing off while Wynne had his nose tucked into what appeared to be a very intriguing novel. All of the other Paras sat in relative silence, the roar of the chopper making conversation challenging. Like many in the British Armed forces,

Mullen had decided to follow a long-standing family tradition. He'd attended the Royal Military Academy in Sandhurst, becoming an infantry officer.

Mullen was a grizzled combat veteran in every sense of the word. He'd seen action in Afghanistan, Sudan, Iraq as well as Eastern Europe. Prior to being sent to North America, Mullen had watched three of his comrades massacred fighting Russian forces in Polish territory. Taking over a small city in western Canada that most of the members of the platoon had never even heard tell of before seemed like a waste of resources to Mullen. He had mixed emotions about this one particular mission. Not that he was a huge fan of working for the UN in the first place. But orders were orders. And he would do whatever it took to keep this section of the republic free of anarchy and lawlessness, even if it meant sacrificing Canadian citizens. He hoped that it would not come to that.

Sitting across from Mullen was Brian Vance, a young private who hailed from the lush green countryside around Nottingham in the Midlands of central England. Vance had a youthful, almost-baby face, like that of a choirboy. He'd sung with the choir and served on the altar at Saint Paul's, his home parish. Bored but at the same time a little nervous about his first mission, Vance, who had just recently completed the rigorous training to be a Para, fiddled with his L85A2 rifle. The novice soldier was aware of all the conflict taking place around him. He had nothing against Americans or Canadians and the thought of having to potentially pull the trigger on any innocent person disturbed him deeply.

Beside Vance sat Peter Huggins, a close friend whom he had known since basic training, was half-asleep.

"Hey Pete." Vance punched his shoulder playfully.

Huggins snapped out of his groggy state.

"Wha...we there yet?"

"Another twenty minutes. Colonel wants us loaded up and ready to move."

*****

Private Brian Vance breathed in the warm, dry air. This was a region of Canada he could never have imagined even existed—an arid, semi-desert area surrounded by high mountains and rife with sagebrush, tumbleweeds and cacti. Vance and the fifty-four other members of the Parachute Regiment had been sent into Kamloops to assist the militarized police forces who were poised to lock the city down completely. They stood at half-attention in front of Lt. Colonel Mullen and his staff officers. The two Chinooks and two Hercules aircraft were grounded on the runway of the Kamloops Regional Airport. Parked in a neat row were the vehicles the Paras would be using while occupying the city: Eight Jackal MWMIK reconnaissance vehicles and four Foxhounds. An additional twenty-five support personnel, mainly logistics and communications specialists, were getting set up in their new headquarters at the airport.

Mullen rubbed the quarter-inch of hair atop his nearly bald scalp before setting the black beret back onto it.

"Good afternoon gentlemen. We don't have much time to get settled into our new home. As our orders stand currently, you men will be working on alternating shifts manning checkpoints on the Overlander and Red bridges, as well as those that cross the South Thompson River on the southern Yellowhead Highway and Halstrom Street. A small contingent will remain on guard duty at the airport here." Mullen cleared his throat. "Captain Wynne would like to speak briefly before you are sent on your assignments."

"Alright men," the tall, stocky British officer barked. "You will be staying in the barracks that have been set up on base for you. It isn't fancy, but according to what officials from the regional government have told us, your living accommodations are only temporary until better ones can be found. It may appear to be a bit of a culture shock, but you will soon get acquainted with the local area. As the predominant United Nations force in the district, you'll sooner or later be working alongside your counterparts in the North American Police. I expect all of you to show the same type of respect to NAP officers as you show to your own."

Being his first mission, Vance was a bit apprehensive. He said a silent prayer to help get him through this trying time.

Chapter 4

His armpits, back and face were nearly drenched in sweat. Jake felt good all over as he finished up an intensive, hour-long workout in the gym he'd set up in the basement of his home. Today's workout consisted of a circuit: ten curls on each arm using thirty-pound dumbbells, ten dumbbell flies as well as ten shoulder presses. He repeated the circuit ten times. Jake took a drink of a double chocolate whey powder protein drink and gulped it back. He then wiped his face.

Jake had spent much of the day tinkering around the house. He was looking into starting up a small handyman-type business. After retiring, he had received a generous pension from the U.S. government. When their father passed away, Jake and his sister received $250,000 that had been hidden away in an offshore account.

It was a sheer miracle the Federal Government hadn't stolen that along with his military pension.

*****

Toombs stood behind two NAP operators that gazed intently at computer monitors. A large communications centre had been set up at the Kamloops Airport. A small group of drone pilots were also posted in a command centre a few doors down the hallway. A look of satisfaction highlighted Toombs' usually cold, unflinching face. It gave Toombs immense pleasure knowing that he was in charge of this large operation and that Frank Carragher had given him free reign to do whatever he wanted.

The door of the communications centre opened. An NAP trooper entered and went over to where Toombs was standing.

"Sir, Mullen is here," he stated.

During his tenure in the United States Army, Toombs had had the opportunity to work alongside soldiers from the British Armed Forces. His family on his father's side were the descendants of farmers from the south of the United Kingdom who had immigrated to America in the mid-18th Century. They had fought for the Continental Army during the bloody conflict that won the United States its independence.

Mullen was the epitome of a serious, by-the-book British officer.

"It's nice to meet you colonel," Toombs said. "You're not the only one who's miles away from home."

"Where are you from? Mississippi? Perhaps Georgia?" Mullen inquired.

"Right from the Heart of Dixie."

Mullen did not know what his North American Police counterpart was talking about.

"Alabama. Colonel, are all of your troops where they are supposed to be?" Toombs asked. "Yes. Once the takeover begins, nobody is entering or leaving this city."

"We will have total control. Exactly as President Asher wants it to be. Have you spoken with the district administrator yet?" Toombs asked.

"Not yet. But very soon."

*****

The air inside the kitchen of Nicole Clare's home was permeated by the mouth-watering smell of freshly-baked chicken. Nicole removed a sizzling pan from the oven and set it onto the counter. Throughout the day, she couldn't stop thinking about Jake. He was becoming such a part of her life that it was difficult to be away from him for even short periods of time. Tonight, after Arielle went to bed, Nicole would most likely do what she did most nights: keep awake well past midnight with the help of an entire pot of coffee and write to the hundreds and thousands of fans who followed her blog.

As Arielle set the table, Nicole noticed two APCs rolling down her street. The fearsome, heavily-armored beasts were parked a few doors down from her home. Nine muscular, burly NAP non-commissioned officers led by a lieutenant got out of each one. They were outfitted in black Kevlar uniforms, helmets and high boots. They carried MP5 submachine guns, M4 rifles and shotguns. Nicole watched in horror, her heart beating wildly out of control, as a bunch of the militarized thugs forced their way into a neighbor's home. Nicole and Arielle stood frozen in terror at the sound of the helicopter rotor blades beating the air into submission directly over their home.

Pale with panic and fright, Nicole reached for her cell phone.

Jake had just gotten out of the shower when he was alerted by the familiar ringtone. He answered it.

"Hey baby. What's going on?"

Her heavy breathing tipped him off. Immediately, Jake knew that something was seriously wrong.

"Jake...Jake" she struggled to catch her breath. "They're...outside on my street. NAP forces."

At that very moment, the door was kicked in. Arielle let out a bloodcurdling scream as four NAP troopers burst inside.

"Jake!"

While two of the jackbooted thugs grabbed a struggling, hysterical Arielle, another trooper, a sergeant, snatched the phone from Nicole's grasp and smashed it against the wall. The sergeant was a mean-looking brute.

"Nicole Clare," the sergeant said without emotion. "You are under arrest for subversive activities."

Nicole's entire body went numb. It was her worst nightmare come to life. The troopers escorted mother and daughter outside. The Carson's, a family Nicole had gotten to know quite well, were being forced onto the back of a military truck, as were eight or so other neighborhood residents.

"Mommy, where are they taking us?" Arielle trembled as she asked.

"I don't know baby," Nicole replied as she held the little girl close to her.

Chapter 5

Fearful adrenaline surged through Jake's veins. It took a moment for the full gravity of the situation to kick in. In his mind, he would love to shoot dead every one of those goons who had just kidnapped the love of his life. In reality, that wasn't going to happen. His mind raced in a dozen different directions. Accustomed to thinking on his feet, still he had no idea what to do. Jake peered out his living room window. NAP troopers were forcing his neighbors out of their homes at gunpoint. He tried desperately to control his breathing.

Jake opened up his bedroom closet. A square metal box sat on the floor. It could only be opened by a biometric code. Inside the metal box was a little parting gift he received after retiring from the air force; a Beretta M9. Despite the total ban on private firearm ownership, Jake had managed to keep the Beretta hidden. Next to the metal box was a canvas bag filled with waterproof matches, a sleeping bag, dried food, fishing line, hooks and sinkers and survival candles. Jake had made the 'bug-out' bag himself. He scooped up the keys to the Dodge Ram sitting in the driveway and quickly went outside.

Two NAP armored personnel carriers parked themselves in the middle of Benton Street. Machine gunners posted in the turrets watched all activity happening around them. Jake discreetly opened up the Ram's doors. All of a sudden a severe voice came out of nowhere.

"You there. Stop!"

Two troopers, their faces partially obscured by the visors on their helmets, approached the driveway. His heart pounding, Jake reached for the handle of the Beretta tucked inside of his jacket.

Jake swiftly ducked behind the Ram, pulled out the Beretta and fired. One trooper, struck in the knee, crumpled to the ground. The other, struck in the abdomen area, fell to the street bleeding profusely. Jake got into the truck, started it up and drove like a madman down Benton Street. The street ended with a barricade of clay hills where suburban homes would one day be built.

Jake revved the Dodge Ram at one-hundred-and-forty kilometers an hour. He practically flew over the rugged terrain of hilly grassland, sagebrush and tumbleweeds that marked the beginning of the 15,712-hectare protected Provincial Park. Jake held on as the $30,000 truck stumbled and lurched over the bumpy terrain interspersed with sections of dry ponderosa pine trees. Since moving to Kamloops, Jake had become quite familiar with the vast Thompson-Nicola region, hunting, fishing and camping every chance he got. Unfortunately, he'd just been taken out of retirement and pressed right back into active duty. Only this time he would be going to war against the very government he once pledged to defend at all costs.

Jake was getting close to a more forested section of the park that would afford better cover. Suddenly, his nerves braced at the sound of an encroaching helicopter. High above, an NAP pilot flew a Eurocopter EC120 Colibri. An observer was watching the fleeing Dodge Ram through a pair of binoculars. Ground units were being mobilized to hunt down and destroy the malcontent. Jake prayed that he would be able to get away before his pursuers sent him into the afterlife.

Chapter 6

"Jake Scribner. Age forty. Address, 58 Benton Street, Kamloops. Retired from U.S. Air Force."

Toombs simmered as the name of the individual who had just murdered one of his troopers was announced over the radio system. The former U.S. Army Ranger was quite concerned that such bold displays of rebelliousness could spark an all-out chain reaction. Toombs and Allister Mullen watched as a group of NAP operators communicated with the helicopter unit that was following the Dodge Ram as well as the ground units that were gearing up to hunt Jake down. Toombs wasn't the only one that had grave concerns. Mullen had heard more than his share of horror stories from both his father and grandfather about the bloody violence in Northern Ireland. It was simply astounding how a relatively small number of Provisional Irish Republican Army fighters had inflicted an incredible amount of pain and suffering on British forces. Canada, with its vast, treacherous terrain, would be prime ground for an effective insurgency to form.

One of the operators, an attractive young woman who had her hair held back in a bun, spoke with the pilot.

"Air Three, where is the enemy combatant headed?" she had a soft voice.

"Northwest. Further into the park," the pilot replied. "We've lost sight of him though."

The operator turned around and spoke to Toombs.

"Major, even if Scribner manages to elude us, he won't be able to get away. We've been tracking him the entire time through his cellular phone."

"Good work corporal," Toombs replied gleefully. He turned to Mullen. "Putting this scumbag out of commission ought to be a relatively straightforward operation."

*****

The underbody of the two-month-old grey Dodge Ram was hanging on by a thread. Jake drove the beat-up four-wheel-drive truck into a hill. He'd reached the end of the line. Before him was a thickly-forested area. He was a stone's throw away from the Mara Hill section of Lac Du Bois Park. Jake grabbed the bug-out bag from the Ram and scooted into a rocky crevice sandwiched between magnificent rugged hoodoos. The incessant buzzing of the NAP surveillance helicopter was within earshot. Jake moved slowly through the crevice. The pilot skimmed the rocky, pine-dotted terrain but was unable to spot his quarry. Jake continued moving until he was into more densely-forested higher elevations of pine and evergreen trees. Soon he would see the peaks of some tall mountains.

A former Canadian Army Bearcat, slightly modified for service in the North American Police, pulled off of the main road that wound through Lac Du Bois. Eight troopers under the command of Staff-Sergeant Ron Huxton exited the back of the vehicle. Among them was Corporal Mike Stephenson, a native of Peoria, Illinois, who'd honed his skills as a dog handler with the Illinois State Police K9 unit.

Short sleeves had replaced heavier clothing in the warm late-April sun, exposing the troopers' chiselled arms. A few troopers had sadistic grins on their faces, as if they took a perverse pleasure in harming innocent people.

Huxton slung an M4 over his shoulder.

"Alright boys," Huxton said. "We're on a seek-and-destroy mission here. We take no prisoners."

*****

The ice-cold water of the bubbling creek was numbing as Jake rushed through it. He immerged himself in as much water as possible in a desperate attempt to wash off his scent so that it would not be detected by pursuing dogs. His uber-fit body was sore but he still had plenty of 'gas in the tank'. Horrific visions of things happening to Nicole and Arielle clouded his thoughts. Then a truly frightening thought popped into his head. He hastily reached into his jeans pocket. His Android Smartphone! The buggers had been tracking him the entire time!

A low, bone-chilling growl! The kind of sound that could paralyze even the toughest woodsman with fear. Slowly, Jake turned around. Standing no more than twenty feet away was the biggest, more ferocious grizzly bear he'd ever laid eyes upon. The beast weighed over a tonne and was clearly hungry. He had two unappealing options: be shot to pieces or become a wild animal's dinner.

'*Come on Jake. You gotta think of something here,*' he said to himself.

The grizzly let out a deafening roar. Jake suddenly had an idea. He quickly opened the bag and took out a carton of crackers. He placed the Android inside of the box of crackers.

"Here you are big guy," Jake said as he flung the carton at the grizzly.

The bear ravenously gulped down the entire carton of crackers - along with the smartphone. Satisfied that he had bought himself enough time, Jake fled deeper into the wilderness.

Chapter 7

Huxton and his team felt a strain in their hamstrings and lower backs as they trekked up a steep hill. All wore heavy Kevlar jackets and carried an assortment of weapons. Corporal Stephenson gripped the black leather leash attached to the collar of Bo, a large German shepherd. The party had been tracking Jake's scent for close to an hour. As soon as they crossed the bubbling creek, it began to dissipate.

The NAP pilot and observer scanned the canopy of the thick forest of spruce, birch, pine and Douglas fir below.

"Air Three to command centre," the pilot spoke into the radio on his helmet. "We've lost sight of the enemy combatant."

Toombs and Mullen looked on edgily as another female operator with a robotic voice responded to the pilot.

"Air Three, enemy combatant has changed direction. He is now moving northeast."

At that moment, Frank Carragher burst into the communications centre. Toombs could sense the furious vibes emanating from the stocky, arrogant administrator.

"Major, I thought you told me you had this entire situation under control!"

Toombs maintained his cool as Carragher came aboard him.

"Sir, I can assure you that this is merely an unforeseen circumstance that will be dealt with swiftly."

"It goddamn well better be." Carragher noticed Mullen standing there quietly. He quickly regained his composure. "Lieutenant Colonel Mullen. My name is Frank Carragher."

"It's nice to finally meet you Mr. Carragher. I hear you're from Montreal. Wonderful world-class city. Been there a few times myself," Mullen said.

"It is definitely a wonder to behold. Colonel, I am sure you and your officers will find your accommodations most fitting."

"We haven't really gotten a chance to get settled in yet Sir," Mullen replied.

"It's a lovely old home. Big too," Carragher said. "Over a century old. Located right close to downtown."

*****

The information the NAP operator had relayed to the pilot was in turn passed on to Huxton. As the team moved in a north-easterly direction through the dense forest, the sunny afternoon sky was quickly giving way to cloud cover.

As the pilot steadied the chopper in the air, his observer could barely make out the shape of a figure below moving briskly through the woods.

"Is that Jake Scribner down there?" he asked.

"I don't know. Who else it would be?" the pilot replied.

On the ground below, a chill permeated the late afternoon air. The troopers began to feel colder.

"Ground leader…" the pilot's voice came through the small radio attached to the lapel of Huxton's vest. "Target has stopped moving. He's directly ahead of you about fifty meters"

The NAP troopers checked over their automatic weapons to ensure that everything was ready to go. They believed Jake Scribner was resting on the other side of a large hill. Huxton looked over at Stephenson and another trooper named Marrs.

"I want you two to go in first. He's probably played out. Even if that piece of garbage wants to surrender, we won't be giving him the option."

Stephenson and Marrs nodded. Stephenson gripped the leash in one hand, a .45 ACP in the other. Moving ever-so-slowly, the two troopers and Bo moved up to the top of the hill. All of a sudden Stephenson and Marrs found themselves face-to-face with a massive grizzly bear that stood fourteen feet tall on its hind legs. Bo started barking viciously at the bear as his handler went numb with shock. With the full force of his left paw, the grizzly crushed Stephenson's face.

Horrified, the troopers unloaded a dozen rounds into the beast's solid body as it advanced toward them. The grizzly moaned in agonizing pain. Its body riddled with bullets and thick, furry coat drenched in blood, the bear took one step forward before collapsing onto the ground.

Chapter 8

Deep in her heart, Nicole knew that her most profound fears had come to fruition. Up until a week earlier, the sprawling correctional institution located on the eastern fringes of Kamloops had held over two-hundred and fifty mostly male minimum-security inmates. Kept hushed by the increasingly state-run corporate media, the federal government had released all of the inmates on the condition that they fight for the North American Armed Forces. The regime in Denver had been working overtime liquidating hundreds of correctional facilities throughout Canada, the U.S.A and Mexico to make room for millions of citizens who'd been deemed 'enemies of the state.' It was designed as a grand system of labor camps and re-education centres that would rival the gulags of the former Soviet Union. And now Nicole was one of countless prisoners in that system.

The short ride across the city by bus had seemed like forever. Upon arriving at the institution, mothers were separated from their children, who were to be housed in a separate wing of the facility. It crushed Nicole to see her only child torn away from her. The entire situation seemed so surreal. Like the twenty other women that were forced to strip and shower under the watchful eye of two thuggish-looking prison guards, Nicole was fraught with paralyzing fear and trepidation. Just as with the North American Police, all correctional agencies had been placed under the control of a single centralized bureaucracy.

The women cringed as the guards threw delousing powder over their wet bodies. Nicole didn't recognize any of them. A young woman, barely twenty, cried uncontrollably. A guard with a sadistic smile on her lips whacked the girl across the back with her baton. She crumpled to the floor. A couple of the prisoners standing nearby tried to help their fellow prisoner but were quickly thrust back by the guards, who waved their batons threateningly.

"Every one of you shut the fuck up!" one of the guards screamed.

The young woman, her face grimacing in pain, slowly got to her feet.

The next stop for these women who would all be living in the same unit was the supply area. Here they were issued grey/bluish sweatpants, t-shirts, sweatshirts, socks, undergarments and Velcro shoes, then told to get dressed Janet Paynter, a stocky guard with the single gold bar of a lieutenant on the epaulets of her crisp uniform, entered. With her intimidating butch expression and short hair she exuded toughness and a penchant for cruelty against inmates. Nicole glanced at Paynter disdainfully.

"Listen up you pieces of rubbish!" Paynter's voice was commanding and forced one to listen. "You have displayed your insolence toward ideals of our federal government and President Asher. You have forfeited all of the rights you previously had. The purpose of your incarceration is to re-educate you, to drive all thoughts of subversion from your minds. Only then will you be allowed to rejoin our grand new society."

Paynter held a list in her hand. She nodded to three other guards who were standing around the inmates.

"These enemies of the state will be housed in H Block. March them there now," she ordered.

Stanford, a baby-faced guard in his early twenties, stood inside of a small pod. Stanford opened a barred gate into the correctional institution's eight units. Nicole had never been inside the former regional correctional facility before. Recently, the fence surrounding the perimeter had been topped with concertina wire. Guard towers had been constructed at each corner of the perimeter. A fifth guard tower loomed over the entrance to the prison. Nicole and a woman in her early thirties with long, straight brown hair and a kindly, angelic face were shown to the door of a cell.

"Prisoner number 78093 Nicole Clare," one of the guards said. "Prisoner number 13607 Bridgette Shaw. Get inside. This is your new home."

The two strangers entered. The cell was small. No more than two-by-three meters. Bridgette's eyes were heavy. Nicole could sense that she was on the verge of breaking down in tears.

"Come on, sit down," Nicole said in a soft voice.

Bridgette and Nicole sat together on the bottom bunk.

"My name is Nicole Clare."

"Bridgette." There was almost no life in the woman at all. Nicole did her best to comfort her.

"My husband had decided to take the afternoon off. The three of us were going to have an early dinner. Our son, Josiah, is nine." It tortured Bridgette to talk about this. "They just burst into our home, grabbed me and Josiah and put us into the back of a truck. My husband was thrown onto the floor and beaten."

Nicole looked Bridgette in the eye.

"Do you have any idea where they could have taken your husband?"

"I have no idea. Josiah is in the children's wing."

"That's probably where my daughter is too."

"What's your daughter's name?"

"Arielle. She's seven. Bridgette, why did they target you?"

"My husband Matt is the pastor of Good News Christian Missionary Alliance Church. He's on record for saying some rather unflattering things about the regime. He called President Asher the

Antichrist. Nicole, they are trying to eradicate Christianity as part of the New World Order. I don't know what your beliefs are, but I truly feel in my heart that we are living in the End Times. I fully expect the Lord to return any day now."

"I can't say I quite share your passionate beliefs. I do believe in God and Jesus though."

"Are you saved?"

"Don't know what you mean by that. I grew in the church. Still go on occasion. Arielle made her first communion recently."

"You're Catholic?"

"More of the cafeteria variety."

"You are married Nicole?"

"I have a fiancé."

"Where's he now?"

"I'm not a hundred percent sure. Knowing Jake, my gut feeling tells me he escaped the city and fled into the mountains. Jake spent twenty years in the U.S. Air Force. He knows how to survive and fight like the devil himself. And I know he will come back to rescue me."

Bridgette turned to her cellmate with inquiring eyes.

"Why were you targeted?"

"I operate a blog called Liberty for Canada. I have scathingly attacked pretty well every federal law enforcement agency in both Canada and the United States. They've probably had me on a watch list for years."

"I'm terrified Nicole. As things stand right now, I'll most likely never see my husband or even my son again. You know what? These demonic fascists can harass and torture me. Even take my life. But my soul belongs to Jesus."

"I admire your fighting spirit, Bridgette. Don't worry. You and I will get through this together."

Chapter 9

As the evening delved into dusk, the warmth of the spring day quickly dissipated. Although his clothing had dried by now, Jake's entire body was racked by chills. He'd been moving fast for a couple hours in a westerly direction, ready at a moment's notice to seek cover from the helicopters and unmanned aerial vehicles that flew overhead. He'd noticed a lull lately. He was not so naïve to think that the authorities would give up looking for him.

Bugs tormented the former Special Operations soldier as he trudged wearily through a marshy area. Jake estimated that he was somewhere between Lac Du Bois and Porcupine Meadows Provincial Park. In others words, in the middle of freakin' nowhere. The last conversation he'd had with Nicole continued to haunt his mind. If she and Arielle were killed, he would track down and mete out retribution all those responsible. He tried his best to cling to the hope that she was alive. And when the time was right, he'd find his way back into Kamloops to rescue both of them from the clutches of those vile monsters.

Jake moved up a rugged hill. He gripped the handle of the Beretta. All nature of dangerous wildlife was lurking out here, including the odd Timber Rattlesnake. Jake caught his breath as he reached the crest of the hill. He hated to admit it, but he was plumb tuckered out. The first thing his tired eyes noticed was a fallen Spruce tree. In survival school, he'd received intensive training in the utilization of natural shelters. He had no tools on him save for a survival knife.

Nightfall would soon be upon the land and he needed shelter- as crude as it may be. Jake zipped open his canvas 'bug-out' bag. He reached inside for the plastic bag containing a variety of protein bars. He took out a large one with four-hundred calories in it. Since making his break into the forbidding wilderness of central British Columbia, Jake estimated that he had easily burned four thousand calories. He desperately needed to replenish his system. He devoured the chocolate chip cookie dough bar. It tasted good.

*****

Unbeknownst to Sarah Jane Pearce and Mallory Hutchinson, life as they had known it this morning had changed forever. The two close friends, who were in their mid-twenties, were alarmed at the volume of air traffic in the skies throughout the day. Rumors circulated that Russian forces had flown over the Arctic and were preparing a land invasion of North America. It was crazy living in a constant state of war. Sarah Jane and Mallory were second-year law students at Thompson Rivers University and shared an apartment. Before commencing a summer internship as clerks with a law firm in downtown Kamloops, the young women had decided to spend a couple of days hiking and camping in the vast wilderness surrounding the city.

Though they were worlds apart culturally and politically, Sarah Jane and Mallory had hit it off since the first day of law school. Sarah Jane, her hair in dreadlocks and always wearing her signature reggae hat and army jacket, was the product of a liberal-progressive family in Vancouver. On her backpack were sewn various logos including one with the symbols of all of the world's religions saying COEXIST, No More Blood for Oil, Women's Right are Human Rights and Give Peace a Chance.

Mallory, on the other hand, was born and raised in a conservative Lutheran family in Calgary. Her father worked as an oilfield executive. Her mother was a housewife who home schooled the couple's six children. Upon graduation, Sarah Jane intended to enter a career doing environmental law for non-profit organizations. Mallory wasn't sure what her career path would be just yet.

The two had been hiking for most of the day and were exhausted. Mallory stopped and sat down on a large fallen tree.

"Sarah Jane, we're going to have to stop for the night."

They had found themselves in a large open area.

"I think we should go on a just little further," Sarah Jane stated as she put her backpack down. "Nightfall will soon be upon us. We will have to set up camp."

Chapter 10

A misty drizzle cascaded from the pitch-dark early night sky. Jake lay in the makeshift shelter, his index finger never straying more than a few inches from the Beretta's trigger guard. Jake flinched tensely at hearing the sound of voices. They were female; young, sweet and heading toward him. Jake slowly got up. He emerged from the fallen spruce tree and ducked low amongst a cluster of bushes. He peered through the semiautomatic pistol's sights. Jake got a good look at the intruders. One was the epitome of the 'girl next door.' The other, with messy dreadlocks, dishevelled clothing and dominant face, fit the bill as being some sort of environmentalist or a women's rights activist. It was obvious that the pair was camping. Perhaps, like him, they'd been fortunate enough to get out of Dodge before the shit hit the fan.

As Sarah Jane and Mallory got closer, Jake confronted them. The law students froze. Standing before them waving a handgun was a ruggedly-built man with a thousand-yard stare and the ability to inflict an abundance of pain and suffering. Like Jake, Sarah Jane and Mallory were also quite distrustful of anybody they didn't know.

"Please…" Mallory, innocent, somewhat naïve to the evil that lurked in the world, trembled frighteningly. "Don't kill us. We mean you no harm. My friend and I were just camping. We saw all these helicopters and planes in the sky today…"

"This is what I've been warning you about Mal," Sarah Jane uttered as she looked disdainfully at Jake, "Violent men and their love of guns and power."

Considering that the federal government now had him on their official shit list, Jake continued to be very guarded. Although he could see that these two lost, scared kids were no threat to him, he didn't want to take any chances until he learned more about them.

"Perhaps you are not aware, but Kamloops has been taken over," Jake stated.

"Taken over?" Mallory asked.

"By North American Police and NATO or UN troops. The city is completely locked down. No one gets in or out. They went door-to-door rounding up all those citizens who are considered a threat to the regime. They kidnapped my fiancé and her daughter."

Mallory and Sarah Jane traded looks as if they believed this dirty, wild-eyed man waving a gun in their faces was truly insane.

"This guy is nuts, Mallory." Sarah Jane turned to Jake. "Look, I don't know what you want. We are no threat to you. Please, just let us leave. We only have a few days until our summer internship begins. We're second-year students at Thompson Rivers."

Jake sighed frustratingly as he lowered the Beretta.

"Didn't you hear what I just said? If you go back into the city, you'll either be detained or killed. If you want to survive, you'll stay out here with me."

"In your dreams, Sicko," Sarah Jane, ever so feisty, shot back at him. "I can just imagine the perverted things you'd love to do to us."

Jake looked over at Mallory.

"Is your friend always this much of a bitch?"

Mallory shrugged her shoulders.

"You can go back to Kamloops if you wish. I'm not going to stop you."

Mallory began to feel less scared. This stranger spoke with utmost sincerity. He had probably just saved both of their lives.

"Sarah Jane, on second thought, I'm starting to think that maybe he's right. I mean, you even questioned it yourself, all those aircraft in the sky today. If I know you, you don't exactly love the current government in power down in Denver, Colorado."

"You really have to believe me," Jake said with a convincing look in his eyes.

Sarah Jane looked at Jake.

"You say you know how to survive out here. Are you ex-military or something?" Sarah Jane asked

"Spent twenty years in the air force. I can hunt, fish…survive out here for a very long time. The first thing we're going to do tomorrow morning is find permanent shelter. Then we have to link up with other groups hiding out here in the forest."

"What is your name?" Sarah Jane asked.

"Jake Scribner. And you?"

"Sarah Jane Pearce. This is Mallory Hutchinson. Jake, what is your fiancé's name? I might know her."

"Nicole Clare."

"The blogger?"

"You've heard of her?"

"I've read some of her stuff. Our politics are as different as night and day." Sarah Jane took a deep breath. "Look, I'm sorry I lashed out at you. You have to understand that we are scared. This is a very frightening time."

"No offense or anything Jake, but we have to get our tent set up," Mallory said. She shivered in the cool evening air. "Which will be no small task in the darkness."

"As you can see, I already have a shelter set up."

"Are you implying that my friend and I spend the night in there with you?" Sarah Jane was very leery. "Don't get me wrong, you're probably a nice enough guy and everything, slightly too old for me. But there is no way in hell Mallory and I are spooning with you tonight."

"Sarah Jane, there is one hard truth that you are going to have to accept; life as we have known it is gone, perhaps permanently," Jake said. "Fate has brought the three of us together. We're going to have to learn to get along. Sure, the idea of getting it one with two hot young women would make most men go crazy with lust. But the fact remains that I love Nicole more than any other woman on this planet. Our sleeping arrangements tonight are only out of necessity."

Mallory and Sarah Jane set their bags down.

"I'm going to assume that you both have cell phones on you," Jake said. "Take the batteries out of them now."

"Why?" Sarah Jane asked.

"It's like this. The federal government and the NAP will be accounting for each and every city resident. They'll take note of all who are missing. They can easily track you through your cell phone. You don't have to destroy them. Just take the batteries out."

Mallory reached into her jeans pocket and took out a Blackberry. Sarah Jane took her iPhone out of her backpack. Mallory showed her friend a small plastic bag.

"We can put our batteries in here," she said to her best friend.

Chapter 11

For Sarah Jane and Mallory, spending a restive damp night in a small shelter with a tall, rugged handsome man whom they'd met by mere circumstance only a few hours earlier felt a bit peculiar but also somewhat comforting. Throughout the night, Jake managed to catch scattered interludes of sleep, but even those were assailed by troubling images of NAP troopers doing unspeakable things to Nicole and Arielle. Early morning light filtered in through the shelter. Groggy, his head banging, Jake turned over and looked at his newfound friends, who were snuggled up against each other sleeping soundly.

Jake flinched at hearing movement outside; footsteps. They were very close. He gripped the Beretta's handle. His body froze as three shadowy figures loomed over the fallen spruce tree. If by some unfortunate circumstances they were NAP troopers or UN soldiers, this party was over. Jake slowly emerged from the shelter. His tired eyes came upon a bear of a man who was a cross between Grizzly Adams and Little John of Robin Hood lore.

Kevin Sorenson displayed little emotion as he aimed a double-barrelled shotgun at Jake's head. Standing on either side of Kevin were two young men in their early twenties. Calvin Sorenson, unshaven and a bit haggard after being away from civilization for a while, had the smooth, appealing appearance of a hot young Hollywood actor or pop star. He gripped a Nosler M48 rifle. The third woodsman, Neil Owlchild, pointed a Lee Enfield at Jake. Neil was Aboriginal-Canadian with long, dark hair and a penetrating scowl. All three were wearing woodland camouflage gear.

Jake could tell immediately that these were desperate men. Jake, Sarah Jane and Mallory had stumbled into their territory, something they didn't take kindly to. He had to tread very carefully...

"Hand off that pistol," Kevin ordered.

Jake tossed the Beretta in their direction. Neil picked it up and stuffed it inside of his jacket.

"You guys from Kamloops?" Calvin asked.

"That's correct," Jake replied. "I barely escaped yesterday afternoon."

"That means the city's under martial law," Kevin stated. "We knew it was only going to be a matter of time."

"How long have you been out here?" Jake asked.

"Since the end of the winter. With all of the turmoil exploding around us we wanted to get out before the hammer dropped," Kevin explained.

Sarah Jane and Mallory awoke hearing men's voices. They exited the shelter. The girls were shocked at the sight in front of them. The three woodsmen lowered their firearms. Calvin smiled lewdly at Sarah Jane and Mallory.

"Hey, Neil. Get a load of this. Appears you and I are going to have ourselves a couple of honeys to keep us warm at night."

Calvin continued to wear the cocky grin as Sarah Jane glowered at him with a look that could kill.

"I would rather be devoured by a bear."

"You've got a lot of attitude, don't you?" Calvin said. "That really turns me on."

Jake and the young women were getting quite hungry.

"I'm going to assume you guys have a cabin somewhere close to here," Jake said to Kevin.

"I've kind of figured out by now you and your lady friends are not government agents," Kevin said. "But we're as concerned about being bothered by looters as we are about the prospect of the government finding our location. I'm sorry, but we can't spare any of our food. It's survival of the fittest out here, understand?"

"You'd be wise not to dismiss me so quickly," Jake rejoined. "I've been hunting big game since I was a kid. Great at fishing too. I can cook as well. I also spent twenty years in the air force."

"What was your trade in there? You don't appear like the officer type to me."

"You're right. I actually worked for a living," Jake replied with a smile. "I was in the U.S. Air Force - Combat controller."

"You a Yank?" Neil asked.

"Duel citizen," Jake answered.

"I spent fourteen years in the Canadian Army. First Combat Engineer Regiment," Kevin stated. "Enjoyed the military for most of my career. That was up until about a year and a half ago. I was on an operation in Syria. I had recently attained the rank of master corporal. I frigged up my leg helping in the construction of a pontoon bridge. Hasn't fully healed yet. This was just prior to the formation of the North American Union. If that wasn't bad enough, the godforsaken government threw me under the bus as it did to most veterans. I received no compensation."

"I was lucky enough to get my pension. I'm Jake Scribner, by the way."

"Kevin Sorenson."

The men shook hands.

"This is my nephew Calvin and his friend Neil Owlchild."

"These upstanding young ladies are Sarah Jane Pearce and Mallory Hutchinson," Jake said.

Kevin nodded to them.

"Pleasure to meet you. Anyway, our camp is about a quarter mile from here. Even though we don't have a lot of food at the moment, I can tell you've all been through Hell and back. Least we can do is offer you breakfast."

*****

As far as Frank Carragher was concerned, the complete subjugation of the Thompson-Nicola District had been a success. Other than the killing of the two NAP troopers, there had been no resistance.

In fact, Carragher, as well as Major Toombs and Colonel Mullen, were astounded by the sheep-like mentality many of the local denizens showed toward their new masters. Carragher stood in his office window peering out into the downtown core and the dry hills and mountains that lay beyond. Toombs stood in front of Carragher's desk. The incidents which had occurred yesterday continued to trouble him. It was unacceptable how the NAP had not planned for every single scenario that could arise in an operation of this magnitude.

Though he was also quite upset, Carragher had largely put the incident behind him. Some veteran who happened to get lucky and was now far from the city was not the most imminent threat to the district administrator's power. As of right now, he had badder fish to fry. The grip Carragher held over his sparsely-populated fiefdom would be ironclad. Any resident wanting to travel more than five kilometers beyond the city limits was required, under pain of indefinite detention, to have an administrative permit authorized by one of his bureaucrats. An 11p.m. – 6a.m. curfew had been put into effect, a curfew that would be enforced stringently.

Toombs simmered in his furious state.

"Sir, we have to continue tracking through the mountains until we find that animal. This district will not be secure until there is a bullet between Jake Scribner's eyes."

Carragher was sick and tired of hearing the NAP officer's bellyaching.

"Major, as I've told you a dozen times already, our manpower and resources are limited. Do you have any idea how many communities are scattered throughout this enormous region I am responsible for governing? Little jerked off one horse towns such as Ashcroft, Barriere, Tranquille…there's over a dozen at least. The main roads are always going to be under surveillance, either by helicopters, drones or armored patrols. The NAP's intelligence division has been working tirelessly to establish a network of informers in each community. In my opinion, Scribner is out there possibly alive, possibly dead. I really don't know. Right now, his sole objective is to survive. He has no reason to want to come back into Kamloops and be a thorn in our side."

"No disrespect, Sir, but you are dead wrong there."

"Explain what you mean by that Major."

"It just so happens that Scribner's fiancé was apprehended yesterday along with her daughter. They're being held at the detention centre. I could be wrong, but I do not believe that we have seen the last of this shit disturber."

"And if this does become a problem, it will be dealt with swiftly. In the meantime, let's not meet trouble halfway."

Chapter 12

Kevin, Calvin and Neil had been hiding out from the authoritarian society building up around them since late February. It was a good-sized cabin situated close to a sparkling lake in the isolation of the Thompson-Nicola region's Bonaparte Plateau. The cabin, constructed of two-by-fours and chipboard and insulated with heavy sheets of Styrofoam, was but a tiny dot in the midst of an endless expanse of forest. Outside of the cabin was a roughly-built shed where two all-terrain vehicles were stored.

The three avid outdoorsmen had driven to the mountains in a Ford Explorer that was parked in the woods at the end of a logging road almost a quarter of a kilometer away from the cabin. They had become quite accustomed to roughing it out in the bush. Their days were spent hunting wild game and fishing for salmon, trout and mackerel. In the yard was a large pile of wood and freshly-caught salmon that hung from a rack ready to be smoked later. The interior of the cabin featured a main area that served as the kitchen/dining room/living room, two small bedrooms and a loft at each end.

Jake, Sarah Jane and Mallory sat with Kevin at the wooden table in the centre of the main area. They sipped strong black coffee from tin mugs. Calvin and Neil had just finished pan-frying a batch of pancakes that had wild blackberries, blueberries, raspberries and even nuts in them. The rebels piled pancakes onto their plates and began to eat. Mallory said a silent prayer to herself.

Jake and the two young women he'd befriended the previous evening dug ravenously into the delightfully-tasting food. It was the first meal any of them had had in close to twenty-four hours.

"So, Kevin," Jake said between bites. "You say you're from the Lower Mainland?"

"I lived in Abbottsford up until a few months ago," Kevin stated. "After getting out of the army, I moved in with my brother, Bob, and his wife, Charlene. They both work-used to work-for the provincial government. Calvin is their only child."

"So where are they now?" Mallory asked as she took a sip of her coffee. "Your brother and sister-in-law, I meant to say."

"Far away from North America. Exactly where I have no idea. Bout' six months ago, they saw the writing on the wall. Decided to pull the proverbial pin. Bob and Charlene had pooled all of their life savings-he's quite a bit older than I am. They purchased a small yacht and sailed out of Vancouver. Figured they could ride out the storm on some deserted tropical island. Calvin wanted to stay behind."

Jake looked over at Neil.

"So Neil, what do you have to say?"

"There isn't much to say really. I grew up on a reserve in the Fraser Valley," Neil replied in a quiet voice. "Katzie First Nation."

"Yeah, Calvin and Neil have been good friends since high school," Kevin stated as he took a drink of coffee. "Played hockey and baseball together. Anyway, it was a difficult decision leaving our world behind. But it had to happen. I can just imagine what those poor folks in Kamloops must be going through right now. Jake, you mentioned something about your fiancé. As I understand it, she was taken."

"I believe so. Nicole called me around two yesterday afternoon." Jake breathed heavily as he recounted the traumatic incident. "Last thing I heard was a bunch of those goons bursting in the door of her house. There was screaming, panic…I don't know what happened after that."

The three outdoorsmen listened to the intriguing story.

"Jake, how were you able to get away without being killed?" Kevin asked.

"I live in Batchelor Heights. When a group of those storm troopers took over my street, I drove like hell into Lac Du Bois Provincial Park and managed to escape. Not before sending two of them to the grave I must add."

The atmosphere in the quaint cabin went from being suddenly relaxed to very tense. Kevin, Calvin and Neil looked upon their guests with circumspection.

"You shot two NAP officers?!" Kevin's thick eyebrows rose in fury.

"That would explain all of those helicopters buzzing around the mountains late into last night," Calvin said with derision. "Uncle Kevin, I knew we were asking for trouble bringing these people here."

Sarah Jane countered, quickly coming aboard the arrogant smartass.

"Don't lump us in here. Mallory and I ran into this cowboy by accident. You have no right painting us all with the same brush." Then Sarah Jane lowered her tone of voice and smiled at Jake. "And if it wasn't for Jake, we most likely wouldn't be sitting at your table right now."

"That would be so unfortunate," Calvin said jeeringly.

"Go fuck yourself," Sarah Jane shot back scornfully.

Kevin glanced over at his nephew with a sombre expression.

"Calvin, I've heard enough out of your mouth for one day."

"Kevin, we cannot allow them to say with us," Neil said adamantly. "If government forces find our cabin, we're all dead."

"I only did what I had to do to survive," Jake said with slight fervor in his voice. "Anybody with any desire not to live under tyranny would have done the same thing."

"He is right," Kevin stated. "Jake, you'll have to excuse my nephew. He often allows his hotheadedness to get the better of him." Kevin moved his eyes from Jake to Mallory and Sarah Jane. "As long as you all are willing to work hard, you're no burden on us by staying here. Actually Jake, come to think about it, there is a reason you and your lady friends came into our lives. I'm not an overly religious man, but I do believe in both a higher power and fate. You're welcome to sleep in the loft located at the left end of the cabin. Mallory and Sarah Jane, the right one is all yours. It isn't fancy but comfortable enough for sleeping. As you can see, we have an outhouse in the woods out there. Now let's get this breakfast finished. We have a lot of work to do today."

Chapter 13

Wracked with worry and fear, Nicole had spent a fitful night lying on the top bunk staring at the bland tiled ceiling. Bridgette had not fared any better. Barring a miracle, they would most likely find themselves locked up in here indefinitely. Following the morning headcount, the twenty women from H Block were escorted to the prison cafeteria.

When they got there, Nicole and Bridgette watched as detainees from the other units sat at long tables eating in silence. Among them was a small group of male prisoners. They picked away at a horrific-looking breakfast of oatmeal, burnt toast, water and coffee. Nicole, Bridgette and two women from H Block who were in their early forties sat down together. Lieutenant Paynter eyed several of the youngest, cutest prisoners. Nicole hoped that she would not have much trouble with the malicious prison officer.

Bridgette said a silent prayer to herself before sampling the oatmeal.

"It's disgusting." Bridgette could hardly stomach the revolting fare.

Nicole took a sip of her coffee.

"The coffee tastes like dishwater."

The two women, Melanie, slim, petite with brown hair And Sharon, a bit heavier with dirty blonde hair, sat there nervously.

'*This type of blatant human rights violation occurs in oppressive regimes such as North Korea or Myanmar, not in what were up until a few months ago two of the freest, most prosperous nations on the planet*', Nicole thought to herself.

"Hi my name is Melanie. This here is Sharon."

"I'm Nicole and her name is Bridgette."

"Nicole Clare?" Sharon inquired.

"Guess I'm a bit of a celebrity in these parts. It's obvious none of us are in here because we broke any genuine laws. What about yourself?"

"When my husband and I were arrested, NAP intelligence agents told us our political activities were a dire threat to national security. We've been quite involved with various environmental causes," Sharon explained.

Her worries never far from her mind, Bridgette looked up from her tray with deep, yearning eyes.

"Sharon, do you have any idea where they took your husband? I have a son who I believe is in here. But my husband, if he isn't dead, is most likely in a labor camp."

Sharon leaned in closer and lowered her voice so as not to draw the attention of the guards that were monitoring them.

"There's one such camp near Banff. Huge. That's where a lot of the men are being sent. Tough conditions. It'll be hell there in the wintertime," Sharon explained.

Nicole glanced at Melanie.

"What about you Melanie?" Nicole asked. "Are you married or have family around here?"

"I'm divorced. Son-of-a-bitch treated me like garbage the entire seven years we were together. Pretty girl like you must have somebody in her life."

"I have a fiancé and a seven-year-old daughter, Arielle. She's in the children's section of the prison. I just hope that I get to see her soon."

*****

Arielle was one of twenty children of adult detainees who were being housed in a newly-constructed wing of the correctional facility-now a re-education centre. The little girl and her fellow prisoners-ranging in age from eight to fourteen-had spent their first night sleeping on bunk beds in a dormitory. Children under eight were sent to live with foster families while many teenagers joined their adult counterparts in the labor camps. Most of the frightened child detainees cried all night for their parents and siblings they'd been so harshly separated from.

There was almost no conversation among the children as they sat at tables in the open area of their unit eating breakfast. A picture of President Asher hung prominently on one wall. His evil, penetrating eyes struck fear in Arielle. A boy with chocolate brown hair who looked to be around eight or nine years old and a girl around Arielle's age sat at the table with her. Tears streaked down the girl's reddish, angelic cheeks.

"Hi," the young boy said quietly to Arielle as he took small bites of his toast.

"Hi," Arielle replied.

"My name is Josiah. Josiah Shaw."

"I'm Arielle."

"I don't know where my parents are," Josiah stated. "I think my mother is here."

"I think mine is too." Arielle had little appetite this morning. She took a few mouthfuls of her oatmeal. It was gross.

Arielle and Josiah looked over at the little girl with red hair.

"It's going to be okay," Arielle said as he placed her arm around her.

"I want my mommy," the child blubbered.

"I want mine, too." Even at her young age, Arielle had her mother's sense of caring. "We can be friends if you like. I'm Arielle."

"My name is Jennifer."

Chapter 14

The palms of Jake's calloused hands sweated as they gripped the two-headed axe. He raised the axe over his head like some warrior in ancient times before driving it with full force into a large block of wood. It split perfectly in two. A glaring afternoon sun hung overhead. It was promising to be another hot central B.C. summer. It had been a few days since Jake, Mallory and Sarah Jane had begun their new life. The members of the small group were slowly learning to get along with each other. Jake and Kevin had really hit it off. The same could not be said about the husky ex combat engineer's nephew. Calvin's arrogant, confrontational attitude was really getting underneath Jake's skin. He had a reasonable tolerance for bullshit, but there were limits as to how much of it he could stomach. On the other hand, Neil Owlchild was friendly and polite, quiet and soft-spoken.

Sarah Jane and Mallory had been out collecting mushrooms, berries and nuts all day. By noon, it had become so warm they were stripped down to tank tops. Sarah Jane wiped a film of sweat from her forehead.

"How are you getting along there Mal?"

The city girl was unaccustomed to this type of physical labor and struggled to keep up with her friend.

"Not much. How am I'm going to adjust to this life?" Mallory sighed tiredly.

"You'll do fine. I'm hoping that we can get a garden planted soon. I've been gardening since I was a kid. Parents always put in a big garden each spring. Love doing it. I've never hunted or fished. Vegan all the way."

Calvin and Neil were involved in the not-so-pleasant task of cleaning bull trout they'd caught in a stream a few hours earlier. Kevin finished patching up a hole in the side of the cabin. Just then, the peaceful afternoon sky was interrupted by the piercing scream of a fighter jet.

"Do you have any idea who that could be?" Jake asked Kevin.

"Either NATO or the North American Air Force. There's been a fair amount of resistance in the border regions."

Not a minute went by when Jake's mind wasn't on Nicole. It killed Jake inside to know that she was somewhere where he could not be with her. But he would rescue both of them come hell or high water.

"I feel somewhat guilty being out here while those bastards enslave and murder our families and neighbors," Jake said with fire in his voice.

Kevin slipped his hammer inside of his tool pouch.

"Jake, what do you suggest we do? Fight back? Not going to happen my friend. Now I can empathize with you about Nicole. And be my guest. If you choose to risk your life to rescue her and Arielle, that's your choice. But you're on your own. We cannot interfere there."

*****

Adjusting to life in her new, hectic and violent surroundings was hellishly hard for Nicole. Being locked away without due process was something she could never have imagined in a million years ever happening in Canada. Slowly, she befriended the other detainees in H Block. Each day was regulated by a strict schedule. In addition to their assigned jobs in the facility, each detainee, under pain of torture, was compelled to partake in daily re-education classes.

Nicole had just finished lunch. As she and Bridgette got up from the table in the cafeteria, a male guard with a flat face, a muscular build and the two chevrons of a corporal approached her.

"Clare." His voice was almost robotic. "Come with me now."

With nervous anticipation, the tenacious writer and blogger was escorted to a small interrogation room. The guard opened up the door. Nicole entered. He locked the door behind her. Nicole shook. Her heart beat fast as she came face-to-face with a man who for years had been reviled by residents of the city.

Ron Storey, a former sergeant with the local police, had recently switched over to the North American Correctional Service's re-education division, acquiring the rank of captain. He was the de facto commandant of the facility. Nicole averted her eyes from Storey's domineering glare. The five-foot-three stocky former mixed martial arts fighter had been the subject of numerous complaints of police brutality and severe professional misconduct.

Two years earlier, when the Liberal/NDP/Green coalition government banned all civilian firearms ownership in Canada, Storey had commanded police, working alongside United Nations Disarmament, Demobilization and Reintegration officers in the door-to-door seizures of guns from Kamloops residents.

Nicole detested the bald, sadistic thug with all of her heart.

"Look who it is," Storey said snidely. "The one and only Nicole Clare. It's nice to finally meet you in person." He pushed a chair away from the table. "Please, make yourself at home."

Uneasy, Nicole sat down.

"So, you think I am, and I quote, 'an authoritarian, jackbooted thug who should be imprisoned for crimes against humanity.'" Nicole felt her blood pressure shoot up. "It's all right there in your blog."

"What's the matter? Hit too close to home?" Nicole shot back at him.

"You've got your father's stubbornness. As it was for him, so it will also be your undoing."

Nicole stood. She towered over the shorter man.

"What did you do to my parents you sick bastard?!"

"Do you actually believe I'm scared of you? Now sit back down or I'll order my officers to do things to Arielle you couldn't even dream of."

Knowing that further resistance would only hurt her at this point, Nicole sat down.

"Your old man as well as your mother refused to go along with the program, if you get my drift. The NAP sent a patrol up to their ranch. Your father rushed outside firing a rifle. What can I say? They were a clear and present danger that needed to be eradicated. Now, on to the more pressing issue at hand. You may or may not be aware, but that fiancé of yours murdered two NAP troopers yesterday as he fled from the city."

Nicole couldn't believe what she was hearing. It was like a dream come true. Jake had not only survived, he'd struck back at the system.

"You're lucky Jake didn't kill more of them."

Storey waved an intimidating finger in her face.

"You're walking on thin ice here Ms. Clare. If you ever want to see your daughter again, you better end this pitiful show of defiance and start cooperating. If you choose to continue your insolence, I will personally ensure that you never see beyond these walls for the remainder of your existence on Earth."

Chapter 15

It had been another exhausting day. As a bright orange evening sun penetrated the west-facing windows of the cabin, the group sat around the kitchen table eating dinner. For the past few days, Jake had been largely unsuccessful in his bid to sell his idea of taking up arms against the district government.

"Jake, I just don't think that you're living entirely in the real world," Kevin said as he took small bites of smoked salmon. "This isn't some Hollywood action flick."

"War, what is it good for?" Sarah Jane was a near total pacifist. "Peaceful civil disobedience is the only way to go."

"More like the most sure-fire way to get yourself killed," Jake countered. "These aren't nice, down-to-earth people who are willing to negotiate. They're bloodthirsty and ruthless."

"You don't think we already know that?" Kevin said. "We only have a few guns and a limited supply of ammunition. Heck, we've been doing most of our hunting with bows and arrows. What good is that against a militarized force armed to the teeth and equipped with APCs, attack helicopters, drones and even fighter jets?"

"Kevin, you were in the military," Jake said. "Surely you learned a few of the basic principles of guerrilla warfare."

"When I was serving overseas, a large part of my duties, especially in the Middle East, was disarming and disposing of improvised explosive devices built by insurgent forces," Kevin explained. "But there's one big thing you're forgetting, Jake. We're living in North America. To be more specific, Canada. Very few people here are used to fighting. Most are just too comfortable. If you're serious about organizing a strong rebellion, you've got your work cut out for you I'm afraid."

"I realize the guy was a butcher who makes Hitler look like a choirboy, but have you ever read 'Mao Zedong on Guerrilla Warfare?' For starters, our enemy will supply us with much of the weaponry and provisions we're going to need. Guerrilla forces dictate the timing of engagement with the enemy. When the enemy advances, we flee." Jake felt as though he was driving his point home. "Save for a few local police, most of these goons are from outside the area. We know this country a hell of a lot better than they do. We will employ Taliban-style tactics; sniper attacks, roadside bombs, sabotage of bridges, highways, power stations…whatever we can do to wear them down. Eventually, we will link up with other resistance fighters and retake Kamloops. That's how the Vietcong were so victorious. They began with small attacks and continued until they were strong enough to launch the Tet Offensive in 1968 along with the North Vietnamese Army. Guerilla warfare is quite possible. You have seen the Red Dawn movies, haven't you?"

"I must say, you're quite a military historian Jake," Kevin said. "But, other than an impossible scenario where we ambush a supply column, you haven't clearly outlined how you plan to acquire the supplies necessary to do this."

Calvin looked over at Kevin. There had been something weighing on his mind the entire time.

"Uncle Kevin, I know of somebody who will be sympathetic to our cause."

Kevin peered at him strangely.

"Who?"

"Shamus O'Reilly."

"You mean that crazy old Irishman who lives in the woods off of the Caribou Highway?"

Calvin nodded.

"That's correct."

"My God, Calvin! If your father knew that you were associating with the likes of that! That nutcase supposedly set off a car bomb in Manchester, England back sometime in the early 1980s that killed four innocent people, two of them little children."

"Kevin, I understand that Shamus may have been involved with the IRA at one time. But he's been living in Canada as a model citizen for decades. He denies those allegations. Shamus is an avid survivalist who's probably got all kinds of weaponry cached around his property."

Jake was becoming interested.

"Calvin, how well do you know this man?"

"Well enough. Neil and I have spent a lot of time in this area hunting. We've been to his home a few times."

Jake looked over at Kevin.

"If there's a good chance he'll be able to help us, we have to at least try," Jake stated.

"I suppose so," Kevin said reluctantly. He looked at Calvin. "The trip will take a few hours heading west. Whatever you do, don't veer off the backcountry trails."

Chapter 16

Throughout much of his childhood and youth, Brian Vance had been a loner. Sure, the young, fresh-faced paratrooper might have played a bit of football or attended the odd party but, by and large, he preferred to do his own thing. Given the volatility of the situation they were in, the Paras were not permitted to go out to local clubs and drinking establishments. On their days off, they were allowed to tour around the city provided they did so without drawing too much attention to themselves. A history buff, Vance found a few things in the ranching and logging town of eighty-six thousand people that piqued his interest. He enjoyed exploring several old churches in Kamloops. The semi-desert climate of the area reminded Vance of one of the areas of the southwestern United States he'd visited while on training exercises such as Salt Lake City or Santa Fe, New Mexico.

It was a pleasantly warm spring day. Wearing a pair of beige cotton pants and a golf-style shirt, Vance walked past tense-looking residents along Nicola Street in downtown Kamloops. He was aware that several people of British descent lived in the city. As of yet, Vance hadn't been the recipient of any hateful stares from the populace. Vance personally didn't believe that the UN, and more specifically, the United Kingdom, had any business oppressing Canadians and Americans, though he was compelled to follow orders under pain of court martial, even death. Vance simply wanted to get his tour of duty over with. In a year's time, he would be home in England. His goal was to leave the armed forces and go to university to become a history professor.

*****

Frank Carragher stood on the deck of the swanky two-storey house that had been seized from its previous owner in the affluent neighborhood of Westsyde. The house, which featured a fifteen-meter swimming pool, offered a picturesque view of the west bank of the North Thompson River, flanked on both sides by hills dotted with ponderosa pine trees, tuffs of grass, cacti and sagebrush. Other high-ranking members of the federal government, including Major Toombs, also lived in homes in the neighborhood.

Though he he'd excelled in his professional life, Carragher failed miserably in the few relationships he'd had with women. He had actually been married once-many moons ago. She was a somewhat hefty woman from the Maritimes who had worked in the same office as he did. Although she had many of the same attributes as Carragher, both of them were too focused on their careers, and thus the marriage ended. Although Carragher had always been bland and uninteresting-at least from the perspective of any woman he'd dated-he lamented the lack of female companionship in his life, or more specifically, a severe lack of sex.

When he was a teenager, Carragher attempted to date girls but was laughed at and ridiculed. His self-confidence destroyed, he turned to pornography, quickly becoming addicted. But now, at this stage of his life, he had been given a position that bestowed vast amounts of power upon him. The type of power that would enable him to get any woman he chose. In order to earn privileges, female detainees selected to sleep with him would have to do so or there would be consequences. It was a gratifying feeling to have this much power and control over others. It was something he had dreamed about his entire life.

Chapter 17

Shamus O'Reilly had lived what seemed like a million lifetimes over the past seventy years. He was born in Belfast, Northern Ireland, the sixth child of a devout Roman Catholic family. It was tough growing up in an area of the city that was predominantly Protestant. Struggling, with no genuine prospects for the future, the disillusioned eighteen-year-old joined the Provisional Irish Republican Army. O'Reilly was assigned to a three-man active service unit whose duties included constructing explosive devices and planting roadside bombs throughout the Northern Ireland countryside for the purpose of ambushing British troops and Royal Ulster Constabulary units.

In 1981, in retaliation for the death of famed IRA member and republican politician Bobby Sands, who had starved himself to death in prison as a protest against injustices perpetrated by the British government, O'Reilly travelled covertly to Manchester, England. His assignment: set off a car bomb in the middle of a busy city square. It was around this time that the IRA veteran began to question why he was even involved in this fight. Like most Catholics in the North, he longed for a united Ireland, but at the same time, he could not bring himself to murder innocent people.

While in the U.K., O'Reilly devised a plan to change his identity and get out of the terrorist organization for good. At the time, many Irish citizens were establishing good lives for themselves and their families in the United States, Australia and Canada. O'Reilly arrived at Pearson Airport in Toronto in 1982 under an assumed name.

The aging Irishman believed that he'd left a war-torn past behind him. But now, as a once-free and prosperous continent descended rapidly into tyranny, images from his childhood and early adulthood came reeling back to haunt him. He recalled with horror the events of January 30, 1972, the Bogside Massacre, forever etched into the memory of the world as 'Bloody Sunday.' On that fateful day, members of the British Parachute Regiment gunned down thirteen Irish Catholics who were marching for civil rights.

For the past ten years, O'Reilly had been living in seclusion in a log home in the midst of the spectacular countryside northwest of Kamloops. Almost completely self-sufficient, O'Reilly rarely ventured out. So far, the authorities had not bothered him. He prayed it stayed that way.

*****

It had been years since Jake had ridden on a four-wheeler. He held on tightly to Neil as the off-road vehicle bumped over the uneven terrain. Jake was hoping that this former IRA operative was truly who Calvin and Neil claimed he was. They drove into the small yard in front of the cabin. The entire property was surrounded by thick forest.

O'Reilly jumped at hearing the faint buzz of engines in the vicinity. It was the distinctive sound of ATV's. O'Reilly was aware of small groups of individuals who lived off the grid in the mountains hunting, fishing, gathering berries and growing whatever food they could. He reached for the loaded .223 standing upright behind the kitchen door. As the two all-terrain vehicles approached, O'Reilly stepped out onto his deck. He aimed the rifle at them.

Calvin and Neil turned off the engines. Jake felt a surge of adrenaline coursing through his veins. He was eye-to-eye with the bushy bearded maniac waving a high-powered rifle in his direction. He certainly wasn't keen about the prospect of being killed out here.

"Turn around and get the hell away from here now!" O'Reilly ordered.

"Shamus, it's us," Calvin said.

"Who are you?" O'Reilly pointed his rifle intimidatingly.

"Calvin Sorenson and Neil Owlchild."

"Remove your helmets…very slowly."

O'Reilly kept the rifle trained on them as they all took off their helmets. He was relieved.

"Oh, yes. How are you boys? Doing much big game hunting these days?" he peered at Jake with suspicious eyes. "Who is this?"

"Shamus, I'd like you to meet Jake Scribner," Neil said. "He's a combat veteran. Been helping us out."

O'Reilly set the .223 down.

"Nice to meet you Jake. You lads might as well come inside."

Jake, Calvin and Neil followed their host inside. Stuffed trophy heads of elk, deer, bear and wild boar were displayed high on the walls of the home's interior.

"Take a seat there, lads," O'Reilly said as he pointed to a couch and two chairs.

Jake noticed that O'Reilly was exceptionally fit for a man of his age.

"I take it you're making a go of it out here in the bush," O'Reilly said. "It's quite obvious you ain't in the city or else you wouldn't be allowed to roam freely."

"Our hideout is a few hours east of here," Calvin explained. "Shamus, the reason why we're here today is…well…we need weapons. We're going to launch a guerrilla war against the system."

O'Reilly's eyes lit up like diamonds.

"Good to hear boys. You know, I'd probably ruffle a lot of feathers by saying this, but I've noticed since immigrating to Canada that many folks in this country are complacent. Hell, the U.S. isn't a whole lot better. Perhaps it's because North Americans haven't known hard times in living memory. Heck, there hasn't been a genuine war fought on continent in over two hundred years. And no, I don't consider the U.S. Civil War to be in that category. It's going to take good people such as yourselves to win our freedoms back. I'm getting a little old for that game but I'll help you any way that I can."

Jake, Calvin and Neil were happy to hear this.

"Follow me downstairs," Shamus said as he opened the door to the basement.

They followed Shamus down a flight of stairs. In contrast to the burning temperatures outside, it was remarkably cool down here. O'Reilly turned on a light. He then removed a false wall. Inside were two AR-15 rifles hanging on a shelf, half a dozen or so boxes of ammunition as well as four brick-sized chunks of C4 plastic explosive, blasting caps and detonators.

"I don't have much. You're welcome to take one of the Armelites, if you wish," O'Reilly stated. "Jake, do you have much experience with plastic explosives?"

"Some. I've used it behind enemy lines before. Calvin's uncle used to be in the Canadian Army engineering core."

"What branch of the service were you in?" O'Reilly asked him.

"United States Air Force. I was a combat controller."

O'Reilly took down one of the AR-15s and presented it to Jake.

"Calvin probably told you that I was in the IRA. We used to have a nickname for these little instruments of death and misery. The 'Widow Maker.' Many of those Royalist bastards met their Waterloo at the end of one of these."

Chapter 18

During his tenure as a priest, Father Julian Tuck had seen his share of difficult times. None were anywhere near as trying as the fiery ordeal his flock was dealing with since their city had been taken over close to a month earlier. Tuck, the rector of Sacred Heart Church, had a large congregation of over one hundred families. Some of his counterparts in the other Christian churches in the city had been apprehended and taken away. Tuck wondered when it might be his turn. At least thirty members of Sacred Heart had been detained.

Tall, with a full head of salt-and-pepper hair, the veteran priest didn't look like he was about to turn sixty. The former abbot of a Trappist monastery in Ontario was an avid cyclist and hiker. He lifted free weights two days a week. His home was on a spacious acreage just outside of Kamloops where he operated a small business raising bees and selling honey.

Tuck had been in the parish office all morning catching up on paperwork. He heard somebody walking inside. Tuck stepped out into the foyer to find Barbara Hunt standing there. Barbara was in her late fifties, had auburn-colored hair and a pleasant face. She and her husband, Robert, were devoted members of the congregation. The long-married couple had two daughters-Molly and Rachel-that lived in Vancouver. She was obviously very worried and anguished.

"Good afternoon Barbara," Tuck greeted her warmly. "How are you today?"

"We're hanging in there, Father," she replied with a weak sigh.

"Please, come into the office."

Barbara followed Tuck into his office. She took a seat on the plush couch. Tuck sat behind his desk.

"How's Robert these days?"

"Tense, as usual. Molly and Rachel are never far from our thoughts. We haven't had any luck trying to reach them by phone or email. I'm worried. I truly am. There's a family that lived next door to us. Robyn and Mike Johnson. They have three children. Last week, the entire family was arrested. Another neighbor of mine disappeared a few days before that. My God, I hope that we're not going to get targeted."

"God will protect us all," Tuck stated. "Mike and Robyn Johnson-I don't believe they are members of Sacred Heart."

"They weren't really religious from what I can see. Mike was the regional director of some national gun rights organization. I know he was very outspoken."

Tuck was aware that some men and women who attended mass on Saturday evenings and Sunday mornings were not practicing Catholics but were in fact government agents spying on and reporting individuals heard expressing subversive opinions. It was quite similar to the Stasi in the former East Germany, or the Soviet KGB. The church building could be bugged. In any event, Tuck prayed solemnly that the Lord would protect his flock from the evil that surrounded them.

"It's heart-wrenching what happened to Bill and Francine Clare," Barbara said.

"There was nothing left of the bodies to even give them a proper burial. Were you aware that their daughter and granddaughter are locked up in the former jail?"

"No." Barbara was quite shocked.

Barbara leaned in closer as if somebody was standing there listening to their conversation.

"Father, I'm about to reveal something that cannot leave this church."

"Anything you tell me is strictly confidential."

"Bob knows a guard who works at the prison. Young fella. Hasn't been there very long. There are several new guards on staff, many of whom are from the U.S. About Nicole and Arielle, have you seen them yet?"

"Not yet. I will have to go through the bureaucratic process of getting a pass. And I don't expect that to be a walk in the park."

Chapter 19

The members of the fledgling guerrilla outfit sat around the cozy cabin having a deep discussion about how they were going to train to prepare for fighting NAP and UN forces.

"Calvin, Neil and myself counted every bit of ammunition we have," Kevin explained. "There are a hundred rounds for the Nosler, two hundred for the Lee Enfield, forty shotgun shells as well as a hundred rounds for the AR-15."

"Uncle Kevin, you forgot about the 10/22." Calvin said.

"Thanks for reminding me. Yeah, we have five hundred rounds for it. Jake, how many rounds do you have for the Beretta?"

"Just whatever's in the mag," Jake replied. "I had to grab it in a hurry. Considering that there is a good surplus of ammo for it, we can use the 10/22, albeit sparingly, for target practice."

"That 10/22 was the first gun my father ever gave to me," Calvin said with a hint of sadness in his voice. "I hope I see my parents again."

Kevin patted his nephew on the shoulder.

"Your father is made of tough stuff. He'll survive." Kevin looked over at Jake. "I was thinking. Considering the circumstances, it wouldn't be unethical to break into abandoned homes, garages, whatever, to find tools, explosives, whatever we can construct IEDs out of."

"It wouldn't be at all," Jake replied.

"Gas stations usually have propane cylinders locked up in a cage," Calvin stated.

Jake looked around the room to make sure he had everyone's attention.

"Our training will commence tomorrow morning. In addition to marksmanship, considerable emphasis will be placed on stalking skills, unarmed combat, archery and combat medicine." Jake looked over at Sarah Jane and Mallory. "Do you girls have any skills you could contribute?"

"I have a major in environmental management with a minor in women's studies," Sarah Jane explained. "Jake, I wish you would realize that I do not believe in war. I have no problem helping out around here as much as I can, but I flat-out refuse to take the life of another human being."

Jake felt his blood pressure rising.

"So you're content to simply hang around here while your fellow citizens are imprisoned and murdered? Sarah Jane, this occupation is not going to be ended by people sitting around a campfire singing 'Kumbaya, Lord'. Every bit of freedom that you currently enjoy was bought and paid for with the most precious currency there is-blood. Rivers of it! I realize that what I'm saying doesn't sound very appealing, but the truth hurts sometimes."

Neil shared some of her sentiments.

"I can definitely sympathize with Sarah Jane. Why would I want to risk my life for a country that has treated my ancestors like garbage and continues to do so to this day?"

"Neil is right," Sarah Jane chimed in. "Not unlike women, Aboriginal Canadians, have always been the object of scorn by evil white men flaunting their privilege and superiority. And who continues to run the governments of most western countries? Evil white men."

Jake had heard enough of her ranting.

"Am I an 'evil white man'? If it wasn't for Kevin and me with our years of military experience, none of you kids would even be alive right now. And Neil, on your point, I too believe that patriotism can be quite overrated. But our fight has got to do as much with nationalism as it does taking back what's ours on the local level. I'm a dual citizen. While I don't give a damn about the corrupt politics on either side of the border, I do care greatly about my community and especially the woman I intend to marry one day soon."

"If we start killing their troops, they'll be after us in no time," Sarah Jane said.

"Sarah, it's only going to be a matter of time before they come after us anyway," Mallory said. "I'm a lot like you. I grew up in a big city. I've only fired a gun once, during a trip to the range with my father. Sure, the prospect of having to take the life of a living, breathing human being troubles me deeply. I certainly don't want to lose my own life. But this is the price that has to be paid."

"We're all in this together Sarah Jane," Kevin stated. "Jake and I have fought in conflict zones all over the globe. The big different this time is that instead of being members of our nations' armed forces going abroad to fight terrorism, WE are the terrorists, in the eyes of the government.. If we can all work together on this, we will be triumphant in the end."

Chapter 20

The front side of Mallory's body felt uncomfortable as she crawled into a prone position. The only thing that separated her from the pebble-strewn ground was a thin mat. Downrange at approximately two-hundred yards were three silhouette targets constructed out of sheet metal and nailed to posts. They glinted brightly in the intense midday sun. The six rebels had driven in the Ford Explorer to an old rock quarry a good ten kilometers away from the cabin. The others looked on as Mallory concentrated through the scope of the 10/22. Her body was fidgety. She was very nervous. Mallory had fired off four shots, all of which had struck rocks or the ground close to the targets. She set the rifle down in frustration. Would she ever get it right? Jake kneeled beside her. Mallory removed her earplugs and looked up at him.

"Mallory, the key is to be completely relaxed. Take a few deep, controlled breaths. Shut everything else out of your mind and concentrate solely on hitting the target."

"I'll try," Mallory replied a bit unenthusiastically. She focused the crosshairs on the middle silhouette. She aimed the 10/22 an inch below the target and fired.

The bullet smashing through metal gave off a shrill zinging sound.

"Do it again," Jake said.

Mallory fired three more shots. Jake raised his binoculars. This time she had hit the middle silhouette in the stomach, solar plexus and neck.

"Not too bad. Not too bad at all." Jake was impressed. "We might just make a fighter out of you yet. You have two bullets left. Try hitting the target on the right."

"Here goes nothing," Mallory said with confidence. She focused the crosshairs on the right silhouette and fired two shots.

Jake peered through the binoculars.

"Holy shit! Two in the heart!"

Jake looked over at Sarah Jane, whose facial expression clearly said; *'No freaking way in Hell.'*

"You have to learn eventually. No better time than the present."

"Jake, what part of 'I hate guns, war and bloodshed' don't you understand? Try all you want. You're not going to compel me to change my convictions and principles."

Chapter 21

It was a lonely stretch of highway that ran north from Cache Creek through a stunningly beautiful countryside of semi-desert and towering mountain peaks. For the second time in a month, Calvin and Neil were outside of the relative safety of their isolated wilderness hideout. The two young men drove the Ford Explorer along the quiet highway. Both were aware they were taking a significant risk just by doing so. Calvin knew of a gas station that was in the area. He just wasn't exactly sure where it was.

"Did you really mean what you said the other day?" Calvin asked his close friend.

"You mean about my disdain at the Canadian government for short-changing First Nations people in this country? You bet I did. I also realize that this fight isn't for any particular country but for our own personal freedom."

Over the horizon, Calvin spotted the towering sign for Gavin's Gas Bar and Convenience Store. As they drove closer, it was apparent that the property around the store was deserted and probably had been for quite some time. Despite being a rather shoddy, slightly rundown establishment, Gavin's did sell a surprisingly good selection of hunting supplies and fishing gear.

"We're going to have to park in back," Calvin stated as he pulled into the parking lot. Guaranteed they patrol this stretch of highway regularly."

Calvin drove the Ford Explorer behind the garage and switched off the ignition. The boys got out of the truck. Neil checked the back door of the garage. Locked! Calvin opened up the back of the SUV and produced a pry bar.

"It isn't like the fuzz are going to swoop in and arrest us for breaking and entering," Calvin said with a laugh as he busted open the door.

"No, they'll just put bullets between our eyes," Neil countered.

The two slowly went inside. Calvin gripped the double-barrelled shotgun. Neil kept the 10/22 at the ready. A dead silence pervaded the building.

"Wonder what happened?" Neil stated.

"I have no idea."

Inside the store were aisles of shelves stocked with chocolate bars, bread, canned goods and even fresh fruit such as apples and peaches.

"We definitely hit pay dirt here my friend," Calvin exclaimed exuberantly. "Start boxing up as much of this stuff as you can. I'm going to see what else the old man has in here."

While Neil placed food in cardboard boxes, Calvin picked out some tools and threaded water pipe from a workshop in the back of the garage. He walked out front where four propane cylinders were locked in a rack. Calvin was ready to bust the rack open when he heard the approaching sound of a vehicle. He rushed inside just as an NAP armored personnel carrier pulled into the parking lot.

"Quick, we gotta hide!" Calvin yelled.

The two rebels hightailed it for the boiler room. Eight NAP troopers got out of the APC. All were armed with carbines.

A trooper wearing the four chevrons of a staff sergeant came inside. Two troopers followed behind. Calvin and Neil held their breath as the three NAP troopers entered. One of them picked up a grocery bag which he then proceeded to fill with chocolate bars. Then they left. The eight troopers got back inside of the APC and pulled out onto the highway.

A huge sigh of relief came across Calvin and Neil's faces as they emerged from their hiding place.

"Man, that was close," Neil said. "If they'd have caught…, well, I don't want to think about it."

"Anyway, let's get this stuff and split."

Wasting no time, Calvin grabbed two propane cylinders. They were heavy, but he only had to carry them a short distance. Neil filled four boxes full of food. After loading up the SUV, they got in and drove away.

Chapter 22

Every pore of their bodies gushed out copious volumes of perspiration. It was a humid, sticky evening. The small band of guerillas was finishing up a stalking exercise. All day, Jake had been instructing his fellow freedom fighters in stalking techniques and the basic principles of Survival, Evasion, Resistance and Escape, commonly known as S.E.R.E. Their hands and faces were smeared with mud, ashes and olive green face paint, much of which had become runny with the humidity. They moved stealthily through the thick evergreen forest in a skirmish line.

"This is so ridiculous," Sarah Jane said unenthusiastically.

"Quiet!" Jake snapped. "If this was real you'd have gotten us all killed by now."

Sarah Jane rolled her eyes. What she wouldn't do to get as far away from here as she could...

"Get down!" Jake ordered.

Kevin, Calvin, Neil, Sarah Jane and Mallory swiftly hit the dirt.

"Alright, everybody get back up."

One by one, the insurgents got back to their feet. They had brought a couple of rifles as well as two wooden recurve bows out into the bush with them for target practice.

"Calvin, I'll get you and Neil to go back to the truck and get that archery stand," Jake said.

All of a sudden, the partisans were alerted by the sound of a vehicle rumbling down the shaky old logging road barely thirty feet away. The group had hidden the Ford Explorer well enough that it would not be easily visible from the road or the air. A dark green United Nations truck stopped in the middle of the gravelly road. Jake felt his heart racing.

"Remember how I taught you how to conceal yourselves," Jake stated with urgency.

The rebels blended themselves into the thick undergrowth as best as they could. Two young British soldiers got out of the truck. The driver, a lance-corporal, lit up a cigarette as his mate, on the verge of shitting his pants, hightailed it for the woods. Controlling their breathing, the insurgents remained perfectly still as the somewhat chunky logistics soldier made a beeline in their direction.

He dropped his drawers and plunked himself down on a log. An enormous sigh of relief came over the man's face as he released the demons. Jake steadied his nerves. He reached for the intimidating-looking combat knife hanging from the sheath on his belt. The others looked on in dreadful anticipation as their leader snuck up behind the squatting enemy soldier. The war veteran placed one hand around the Brit's mouth then slit his throat with the other. An ocean of warm dark blood oozed from the gaping cut. Mallory, Sarah Jane, Calvin and Neil were mesmerized by the gruesome sight.

"Ho…ly shit!" Neil could barely get the words out as he watched the young soldier, who wasn't much older than he and Calvin, topple over onto the ground.

The driver stamped the butt of his cigarette out on the ground.

"Martin, what in the name of God you doing in there, mate? I'm telling ya, you have to lay off that greasy shit." He waited another minute. "Martin, you okay mate?"

Concerned, the driver reached into the front seat of the truck and retrieved an L22A2 rifle. He entered the forest. Kevin took short, controlled breaths as he pulled back the bowstring of the recurve bow he'd owned for years. The lance-corporal raised his rifle at hearing a rustling-of-bushes sound. He caught a fleeting glimpse of the well-camouflage guerrillas. Before the lance-corporal could react, Kevin unleashed the bowstring. The wooden arrow sailed through the air, stabbing directly into the man's solar plexus. The driver collapsed to his knees, the life quickly fading from his eyes, before falling over.

"Quick, let's see what's in the back of that truck," Jake said enthusiastically as he picked up the fallen soldier's L22A2.

Jake and Kevin lifted up the flap of the truck while Calvin and Neil searched the cab. Inside the back was a treasure trove of weaponry; a L108A1 light machinegun, four LAW antitank weapons, a crate of grenades, a box with two night-vision scopes inside as well as four large cartridge boxes of 7.62 rounds for the machinegun. There were also several cardboard boxes of meals-ready-to-eat.

"Christmas came early this year," Jake said.

"I hope we can squeeze all of these goodies into the back of the Ford," Kevin replied.

Calvin and Neil found another L22A2 assault rifle in the cab of the truck.

"Hey Jake," Calvin said. "How do you plan on disposing of this truck?"

Jake hadn't fully thought that through.

"There's a ton of muskeg up near Barrett's Lake," Jake said as he turned to Kevin. "They'll never find it in there."

"That's the only logical thing I can think of," Kevin replied. "It will sink in to that muskeg really good. We just have to disable all of the GPS and tracking equipment beforehand."

*****

Three hours had passed since the British Army's contingent in Kamloops had dispatched a truck carrying a load of guns and ammunition to the satellite post in Merritt, close to ninety kilometers away. It had not yet reached its destination and Alistair Mullen was itching to know why. Mullen stood in the communications centre at the Kamloops Airport. Two British Army operators worked alongside their NAP counterparts. Mullen had just spoken with the lieutenant who was in charge of the Merritt outpost. There had been no communication with the driver whatsoever. A Eurocopter EC 135 had been sent out to search the vast mountainous region for the missing supply truck.

One of the operators, a young female private, turned around.

"Sir," she said to Mullen. "It would appear that the truck's global positioning system has been turned off or deliberately tampered with."

'*What the heck is going in?*' Mullen thought to himself. The prospect of that much weaponry falling into the hands of insurgents troubled the veteran army officer. And what of the two soldiers inside? There was ample space out there to not only hide bodies, but an entire vehicle as well.

"Any word from the pilot?" Mullen asked.

"Afraid not Sir," the female operator replied. "No sign of anything yet."

"I cannot believe that a truck has just disappeared without a trace." Mullen was flabbergasted. "All we can do is keep searching for it." Deep down, Mullen suspected that something much more sinister than met the eye was taking place."

Chapter 23

Each day was spent fishing, hunting and gathering nuts, berries and wild plants. The deep-woods partisans had also begun to conduct extensive reconnaissance missions, scouting out the locations of checkpoints and outposts used by the North American Police and United Nations forces. The troubling events from a few weeks earlier continued to bother everyone except for Jake and Kevin. It had been the first time in his life that Kevin had killed another human being up close and personal.

Though she worked hard to keep her mind and body in good shape, the turmoil happening all around her started to weigh down on Sarah Jane's psyche. She just wanted to maintain her sanity until this nightmare was finally over. While waiting for dinner to cook, the six members of the budding insurgency sat around the cabin.

"We're going to begin launching our attacks soon," Jake stated. "People, this is truly the point of no return. We are about to stir up a very angry hornet's nest."

Mallory had been practicing her marksmanship skills as much as the group's limited ammunition supplies would allow her to.

"Jake, I feel that I'm ready to fight."

Sarah Jane turned to her in dismay.

"Mallory, what's going through your head? There is absolutely no reason for you to want to risk your life."

"Then what is worth risking our lives over?" Jake asked Sarah Jane point-blankly. "For far too long in the United States and Canada, the general public has been far too complacent. All throughout the last four or five decades most people have had the 'it can't happen here' mentality. Why do you think we're in this mess now?"

"It's because of lefturds like this granola-munching hippy," Calvin exclaimed with a smartass grin."

Sarah Jane had reached her breaking point with Calvin.

"I swear to God. If you don't stop this I'm going to…"

Jake glanced at him.

"You're really starting to get on all of our nerves Calvin. I'd seriously advise you to quit while you're ahead."

Sarah Jane felt as though her best friend was turning against her.

"Mallory, why are you siding with them?"

"Sarah Jane, to be completely honest with you, I never would have imagined that during the prime of my life, when most people get their education, travel the world and look to the future with optimism, I'd be fighting to survive in the mountains of British Columbia. But here I am. Here we all are. At heart, I'm not a natural warrior. But I realize that if we don't take a stand, risk our lives, that there won't be any future anyway."

Sarah Jane sighed disgustedly at Mallory.

"I don't care one iota about this North American Union. To me, Canada will always be Canada, a sane nation that isn't notorious for its corporate greed and lax gun laws. The Second Amendment? I'll take our free health care and social programs over that any day."

"If you hadn't have been texting your boyfriend during law history class you'd have been shocked to discover that the 'right to keep and bear arms' is not an exclusively American right," Mallory stated. "It originates in Anglo-Saxon common law and is enshrined in both the Magna Carta and the English Bill of Rights. Those two documents are part of the Canadian constitution."

Jake was very impressed.

"Geez kid, you know your history. And I thought my uncle Alfred was good. As for you being ready to fight, we'll have to take a wait-and-see approach there. But at least you're eager so that's a good thing.

Chapter 24

A knot formed in the pit of Father Tuck's stomach. He slowly approached the guardhouse attached to the fence that surrounded the re-education facility. Forty or so family members and friends of those locked up inside stood vigil outside of the fence. A vigilant tower guard toting an AR-15 monitored them closely. Tuck displayed his laminated pass to the stone-faced federal correctional officer inside the guardhouse. After scanning the pass, a second guard escorted the veteran clergyman through the security gate into the administration area of the facility.

A buzzer sounded. Another barred door slid open electronically. It led into the foyer of the sprawling former provincial jail. The veteran priest didn't recognize any of the prisoners walking past him. Their eyes were downtrodden; devoid of hope. Tuck was escorted down a corridor where Ron Storey stood outside the door of a meeting room.

"Good day, Father," the dictatorial goon said in a snide tone. "I think it's safe to assume that you have no intention of smuggling any illicit items into this place. Just to let you know, Nicole Clare is one or our more 'dishonorable' prisoners."

Tuck had never met Ron Storey before, but from the stories he'd heard, this was one malicious individual.

"She's a child of God. The same as every other person who has been wrongly imprisoned in here."

"Says you. I wouldn't get too cocky there, padre. You're being kept on a short leash while inside my prison."

"May I see Nicole now?" Tuck just wanted to get this visit over with.

Storey opened the door to the small room.

"You have twenty minutes. After that, this hated enemy of the people goes back to her cell and you get the hell out of here."

"Thank you captain," Tuck said a bit begrudgingly as he entered the small room.

The door was shut behind him. The officer stood rigidly outside. Nicole sat at the other end of the table. The young woman appeared as though she had been through Hell and back. Her hair was uncombed and dry. Conspicuous, heavy bags hanging underneath her eyes was proof of a lack of sleep. She was pale and weak. Tuck sat down. He held her hand in his.

"I'm so glad that you came, Father."

"It took a bit of bureaucratic wrangling to get in here. Anyway, how are you?"

"It's been one nonstop nightmare," Nicole said tiredly. "I know that Arielle is in here. Those bastards won't even let me see my own daughter!"

"I inquired-I meant, I wanted to see her but the answer was a resounding no," Tuck explained. "It would appear that the goal of the federal government is to completely brainwash impressionable little minds. Therefore, there can be no outside influence."

"If that isn't a bad enough blow, every moment of every day I'm thinking about Jake. I do know that he escaped into the mountains." A sudden smile lit up her unhappy face. "And that he wasted two NAP officers."

"I'm afraid I don't have any comment on that. As a member of the clergy, I am forbidden to partake in the shedding of blood. As is said in the sacred scriptures, there are many wolves, as well as sheep. Perhaps Jake Scribner is a good example of the proverbial 'sheepdog.' We just have to pray that this fiery ordeal ends soon-and peacefully." Tuck hated to see Nicole suffering in the state she was in. "Regardless if any government agents choose to be in my church or not, this Sunday, I will instruct all of the congregation to pray for you, Arielle and Jake. I'm sorry about your parents. I will also pray for the repose of their souls."

At that moment, the door opened.

"Time's up, padre," Storey said as the other officer entered.

Nicole rose to her feet. She held out her arms as the officer handcuffed her wrists.

"Hang in there Nicole," Tuck said to her as he left. "We're going to get through this."

*****

Colonel Mullen continued to wonder if those two young privates, Randall Williamson and Cory French, had fallen prey to the savages that lurked out in the untamed wilderness far beyond the confines of Kamloops. As bright afternoon sunlight reflected off of the small gathering of tall office buildings in the city's downtown core, Mullen and Toombs stood in Frank Carragher's office. The Machiavellian administrator sat behind his imposing desk.

"Sir, as I've been trying to say all along," Toombs said. "Those young men didn't go AWOL. They fell victim to the same maniac who slaughtered two of my men!"

"Major, you have no proof of that. There are still several residents from the district unaccounted for. Everybody around here hates us. For all intents and purposes, Jake Scribner is out of our lives."

"Sir, if I may be blunt, if we allow Scribner to get away with what he did, we'll never gain complete control. I have requested more personnel. We've been using unmanned aerial vehicles. They work fine in the open desert but are woefully inadequate in this type of terrain."

"I've spoken with General Rogers in Vancouver as well as the North American Armed Forces Command Northwestern Division in Seattle. Insurrections are springing up from one end of this continent to the other. As you're well aware, manpower can only be stretched so far. Now, there are most likely a few brigands out there who believe that they can take on the most powerful government in the world right now. Let them enjoy their fantasy. As long as the residents of the Thompson-Nicola district are obedient and don't display any outward signs of rebellion, we can rest relatively easy," Carragher said.

Chapter 25

The name was appropriate for this bone-dry region of B.C. that often got hellishly hot in the summer months. Jake and Mallory were exhausted after spending what seemed like forever trekking through the high desert country and hoodoos of the Deadman Valley. The heavy Nosler rifle was slung over Jake's left shoulder. Mallory carried one of the British assault rifles. The sniper/spotter team had set out from their camp the day before, spending the night in the forests of the nearby mountains.

But now, they were exposed to enemy air patrols in this area littered with cacti, sagebrush, tumbleweed, Big Galleta and Desert Needle. They'd changed out of woodland camouflage fatigues into ones with a semi-desert pattern that featured a blend of different browns, dark and lighter shades of green. Having to be creative and work with what they had, the rebels painted camouflage patterns of khaki, green and tan shirts, jackets and pants they had looted from abandoned homes.

"Remember, shoot and scoot," Jake said in almost a whisper.

"How long before they start coming after us?"

"Five to ten minutes. Once an attack like this happens, ground forces immediately call in air support. It will most likely be attack helicopters. I can't see fighter jets."

Mallory's body felt weak. Her mouth was dry and not because of the burning desert sun. She was getting nervous having to kill another human being for the first time.

"How exactly do you know this?"

"That was my MOS in the United States Air Force."

"MOS?"

"Military occupational specialty. Combat controller. I was often attached to infantry as well as Special Forces units, especially in Afghanistan."

On the outskirts of Cache Creek, where two Trans-Canada highways converged, six North American Police troopers manned a checkpoint. Jake and Mallory crouched down in front of a collection of large boulders in the arid hills surrounding the town. The rebels watched as the troopers stood around looking bored, the blistering hot sun ravaging them in their jet-black fatigues, heavy-plated bulletproof vests and Kevlar helmets. An armored personnel carrier was parked along the shoulder of the highway.

Mallory's heart beat so fast she thought it would jump out of her rib cage. Jake set the Nosler rifle, which was attached to a bipod, on a flat boulder. He adjusted the scope to four hundred yards. Mallory crawled into the prone position, securing the rifle butt firmly against her right shoulder. Due to her nervousness, Mallory found it particularly difficult to concentrate through the crosshairs. Shooting at metal targets was one thing, but standing out there on the highway were six living human beings. And she had to make the ultimate decision which one would be returning back to their family in a cadaver bag. Although deep down the devoutly Christian woman knew these were bad people that would kill her in a heartbeat, she still had difficulty psyching herself up to take the shot.

Jake peered through a set of binoculars. He studied the ranks of the troopers. One standing next to the APC wore the single bar of a lieutenant. The man, early forties with salt-and-pepper hair, doused his forehead with water before taking a long swig.

"See that one standing next to the vehicle?"

Mallory moved the rifle around. She fixed the crosshairs onto the upper chest of the man.

"He's the highest ranking one in the group." Jake sensed her nervousness. "Mallory, just remember what I told you. Relax your entire body. Take three or four deep breaths."

Mallory gently squeezed the trigger. Before she knew it, a shot rang out followed by a deafening crrackkk that echoed amongst the nearby canyons and valleys. The lieutenant crumpled to the ground. Two of the troopers rushed to his aid while the others pointed their weapons in all directions.

Mallory, though a bit shaken, was surprisingly calm.

"It's that time," Jake stated. "We gotta vacate the premises this second."

Jake and Mallory slowly slunk away from their position. As the sniper/spotter team began moving at a faster pace through the desert, their adrenaline skyrocketed at hearing the sound of an approaching helicopter.

"We're not going to make it to the forest in time," Jake said. "Quickly, take cover."

The two insurgents concealed themselves as best they could amongst a cluster of juniper and ponderosa pine trees. Jake glanced up as an Apache attack helicopter ripped through the clear blue sky overhead. He was concerned about how long they would be forced to hunker down out there before it was finally safe to get on the move again.

Chapter 26

Jake and Mallory were at the point of running on fumes as they trudged wearily through the unending mountain wilderness. Dusk was setting in. On a couple of occasions over the past five or six hours, the rebels had had to conceal themselves in the bush as NAP helicopters scoured the ground trying to locate them.

"Hopefully we'll make it home tonight," Mallory said weakly.

"I hope so too. Not too struck on spending another night under the stars. Anyway, let's rest for a minute."

Jake and Mallory plunked themselves down on the forest floor. The forest floor was soft and covered in a blanket of pine needles. Mallory was beginning to have second thoughts about what she had done.

"It is my sincere hope that that man was a Christian. It would crush me to see anybody, even an NAP officer, spending eternity in Hell."

"That's exactly where each and every one of those bastards belongs," Jake rejoined. "Seriously Mallory, those jackbooted thugs invaded our city, killed innocent civilians, suspended Habeas Corpus and the most pressing issue weighing on your mind is whether that piece of shit is in Heaven? Come off it. I'm not religious per se, but I do know that any true Christian would not be party to such evil."

"Jake, do you believe in God at all? Were you ever a member of a church? I was raised in the confessional Lutheran faith, Lutheran Church Canada on this side of the border. We're conservative but keep some of the liturgical traditions from Catholicism. We strongly believe in the Bible and are strongly opposed to such things as same-sex marriage and abortion."

"That's good to hear." Jake, dog-tired, was hoping that he would be able to catch his second wind. "I'm a lapsed Lutheran. Haven't been to church in ages. Parents took my sister and I growing up. That is until they divorced. Don't get me wrong. I do believe in a higher power but I just cannot, for the life of me, get into organized religion."

*****

Kevin had spent a good portion of the day constructing a timer with a fuse attached that could be set off via cellular phone. The fuse would enter through a small hole drilled into a foot-long piece of threaded water pipe. It would then be attached to a propane cylinder. While Calvin and Neil cleaned up the kitchen, Sarah Jane was getting tired washing clothes and old-fashioned way. That is, washing them in a metal tub and hanging them out on the clothesline in the yard to dry.

"How are you getting along?" Kevin asked her.

"Not too bad," Sarah Jane replied.

"Do you still have your cellular phone?"

"Of course. We just took the batteries out of them as Jake had instructed."

"I'm going to need one of them."

Sarah Jane went out into the sheltered yard and began clipping the soaking-wet clothes to the clothesline. It was a warm, dry night. Stars dotted a pitch-black sky. Sarah Jane flinched at hearing a sound coming from the forest. The shadows of two individuals emerged into the open. Sarah Jane's eyes lit up with joy when she saw who it was.

"Mallory!"

Before a worn-down Mallory even knew what was going on, her best friend rushed over and hugged her. It felt good to be back home safe.

"I wasn't sure if you were coming back or not," Sarah Jane said.

"We got our mission accomplished. Got my first ever kill."

Sarah was immediately turned off.

"Mallory, what's gotten into you? You're not the same person I met two years ago. It's like you're becoming violent."

"Sarah, regardless of how things work in your airy-fairly little world, we are currently at war," Jake stated. "I watched as Mallory took out that NAP lieutenant. She did a damn fine job of it too."

Kevin, Neil and Calvin walked out of the cabin.

"I see you made it back in one piece," Kevin smiled as he greeted Jake.

"We made it out of there by the skin of our teeth. But other than that, everything is peachy. And you? How did you fair out?" Jake asked.

"I got the pipe bomb and timer finished," Kevin stated.

"Kevin, I've been giving this quite a bit of thought. As you well know, we aren't going to stay in this one location forever. Considering that we've already poked the proverbial bear, we're going to have to relocate-and soon."

"Where do you think is the best place to go?" Kevin asked.

"Up north. Possibly in High Lakes Basin or one of those provincial parks. Plenty of caves in that area to protect us from the enemy's infrared capabilities."

"Yeah, I guess we are going to have to do that," Kevin replied. "It would be wise to start planning now."

Chapter 27

Calvin and Neil had been working since the middle of the night digging a large, rectangular-sized hole next to the warm asphalt of the Trans-Canada Highway. It was two-and-a half-feet deep. After that was finished, the duo ever-so-gently placed a propane cylinder with a large pipe bomb attached to it inside. An antenna was fastened to the timer on the pipe bomb. Calvin and Neil covered the entire improvised explosive device with sandy soil until only the top of the antenna was sticking above the ground.

Calvin and Neil crouched out of sight atop a hill that offered an expansive view of the highway and the arid hills and mountains that lay beyond. Reconnaissance missions proved that this particular stretch of highway was frequented by NAP and UN patrols. Calvin grasped an L22A2 which had been taken from one of the slain British logistics soldiers. Over the past few weeks, the budding actor and model had found himself becoming considerably less cocky and arrogant than was his normal self. Calvin only hoped that this terrible conflict wouldn't make him too callous.

The two close friends sat in tense silence. Both Jake and Kevin had instructed their younger protégés about the importance of not talking, eating, smoking, etc. in an ambush zone and the grave consequences for doing so. Out of the blue, a lone Humvee appeared. It was camouflaged and had the UN logo on its side. Two British paras sat in front. A third was positioned in the turret manning a massive machinegun.

Calvin held Sarah's phone in front of him. He dialled a number as the Humvee came within a few meters of where the IED was planted. Seconds later, the ground erupted with a sharp explosion that tore mercilessly into the side of the Humvee. Amidst the confusion, the driver lost control of his vehicle. The Humvee struck a guardrail, flipped over and descended down a steep hill to the gulley below.

"Let's make tracks," Calvin said.

The two young, very athletic fighters retreated into the dense spruce forest that blanketed the mountains. Once they'd been running for quarter of a kilometre or so, they heard the familiar sound of a searching helicopter. Hearts racing, Calvin and Neil stopped briefly, jogging lightly on the spot as they took deep, controlled breaths. About a minute later, they continued running.

Calvin had heard stories from his uncle about the NATO missions he'd served on in Afghanistan. Much of the country was mountainous desert and many of the operations carried out against Taliban forces were in open areas. Being in British Columbia, this particular group of freedom fighters had the advantage of mountains and massive forests. After they'd been running for another twenty minutes or so, Calvin and Neil had to stop again. They were almost completely out of breath and sweated profusely. The all-terrain vehicles they'd driven in were not too far away, but reaching them without getting killed would be a challenge.

"I guess we planned this as best we could," Neil said.

"We did," Calvin replied. "Now let's get out those foil blankets."

"You think those will actually work?"

"According to Jake, they block a person's body heat from being detected by infrared sensors."

Calvin and Neil unpacked two foil blankets that were inside of a small bag Calvin carried. The two rebels concealed themselves in the thick underbrush and covered their bodies with the blankets. As evening set in and the ever-present sound of probing helicopters dissipated, the duo dared to venture out into the wilderness. Calvin and Neil moved through a swampy area of thick black spruce where buzzing insects harassed them at every turn. They even had a brief encounter with a bull moose. Luckily the moose had no interest in tussling with two heavily-armed guerrillas and went in the other direction. It was approaching dark by the time Calvin and Neil got back to the ATVs. Slowly, they drove through the narrow backcountry trails praying that the worst was behind them.

*****

Major Toombs stood on the tarmac of the Kamloops Airport. His short-sleeved buttoned shirt offered slight relief from the sweltering night. Toombs stood alongside Colonel Mullen, Lieutenant Brown and Captain Wynne. The four officers looked on as the lights of a North American Police Bell helicopter flew in over the mountains and landed on the tarmac. Mullen, Brown and Wynne were beside themselves in shock at the deaths of the three paras who'd been killed by the roadside bomb.

Seven NAP troopers and a lieutenant named Harvey departed the helicopter.

"Sir," Harvey said to Toombs. "We cannot find any trace of enemy combatants in the area at all." He looked over at Mullen. "Colonel, I am sorry for the loss of your men."

"This is just fucking wonderful!" Toombs was about to blow his top. "I swear to God. If that pencil pusher who revels in telling me how to do my job doesn't soon bring more reinforcements in here, I will pull every one of my troops out of Kamloops and hunt down those savages myself!"

Chapter 28

Robert Hunt peered out of the large picture window in his living room. Hunt and his wife Barbara had purchased the early 1980s-era one-storey bungalow nearly twenty years earlier when he had been posted to Kamloops. For a man in his early sixties, Hunt was incredibly active and energetic. Seven years earlier, the Brandon, Manitoba native had retired from the Royal Canadian Mounted Police after thirty-five years of service. He'd attained the rank of staff sergeant. Like many of his fellow countrymen and women, Hunt resented not being able to live freely in the great nation of Canada he'd grown up in. The retired Mountie was especially incensed when the historic law enforcement agency that had been such a part of his life for so long was merged into the North American Police.

Neither Hunt nor his adoring wife of forty years could have ever foreseen such an extreme shift coming. It was no secret that the majority of elected representatives on both sides of the 49th Parallel had been deceiving the public for years. In Hunt's opinion, the downward spiral had begun back in the late 1980s/early 1990s with several free trade agreements. Integrated border security came into place in the years following the horrific events of September 11th, 2001. As a true-blue Canadian, Hunt had never trusted the United States government. The constant wars, increased surveillance, an almost total loss of civil liberties were part of a grand scheme orchestrated by a twisted, almost Luciferian cabal of global elites, powerful, ruthless evil men that had been bringing tyranny to regions of the world for centuries. Now it was North America's turn to be oppressed.

It had been around the time he retired from the RCMP that the U.S.-Canada border was erased. The then Liberal government in Ottawa succumbed to pressure from Washington to permit American law enforcement agencies as well as military forces on Canadian soil. Before most people could even fathom what was taking place, Canadian sovereignty was all but a distant memory. These days, Robert and Barbara mainly kept to themselves although they occasionally visited with neighbors and friends. Since the occupation, many citizens had become more withdrawn. The atmosphere in the entire city was rife with paranoia and fear.

As a steady rain pattered against the east-facing windows of the home, the Hunts sat quietly sipping tea. Suddenly, there was a knock at the door.

"I wonder who that could be," Barbara asked.

Robert Hunt got up off of the couch and opened the front door. Marty Smith, a good friend of the family for over a decade, stood on the doorstep. Smith was younger, in his mid-forties, tall and wiry with bushy hair and an early 1980s-style moustache. Smith and his wife Marsha lived two doors down from the Hunts.

"Marty, I haven't seen you around in a while. How are things?"

"Being held together," Smith replied. "That's about it though. Mind if I come in?"

"By all means."

Hunt stepped aside as his close friend entered. Barbara got up off of the couch.

"Marty, long time no see," she said happily. "Would you like a cup of tea?"

"Ah, no thank you Barbara." Smith turned to Hunt. "Mind if we talk alone for a minute?"

"I guess so. Do you want to go downstairs?"

"That would be great."

Hunt and Smith descended a flight of stairs into the home's furnished basement. Since the start of the occupation, the local government had established a snitching program. Spurred on by generous incentives, people gladly reported on their neighbors. This resulted in an increasing number of citizens either locked up or shipped to forced labor camps. Over three-and-a-half decades as a cop, Hunt had gained enough wisdom not to trust many people. He had known Marty Smith, who had spent ten years in the Canadian Air Force as a helicopter pilot, for as long as he'd lived in Kamloops. He'd also made sure that the home was free of electronic bugs. The men sat down on a couch.

"So what's on your mind, Marty?"

"Bob, how can I say this? It's time. I am sick and tired of sitting around wondering which one of us is going to be next."

Smith's words struck a nerve inside of Hunt. Was there a chance that his long-time friend could be an informant?

"You're advocating that we start an insurrection. Am I right?" Hunt asked.

"What other choice do we have? Besides, the rebellion has already started. Those guerrilla attacks taking place in the mountains west of the city. Rumor has it some former Special Forces guy from the States is leading a small group of fighters."

Hunt could sympathize with his friend. At the same time, he knew such talk was dangerous and could get them in a world of trouble.

"Who else have you spoken to about this?" Hunt asked, very concerned.

"A couple of guys who I've known longer than you," Smith answered.

Hunt sat back in the couch. It was all too much, too soon.

"I don't know about you, but I'm getting a little long in the grain for that kind of thing. But if we're going to do this, there can be no more than four or five people in a group. As well, everyone will be sworn to secrecy. Not even our own wives can know what we're doing."

Chapter 29

The district government had mobilized the NAP to carry out an aggressive campaign in which any and all potential insurgents living off the grid in the vast region would be rooted out and killed. Heavily-armed strike teams dressed in camouflage fatigues, Kevlar vests and toting an array of weaponry penetrated deep into the rugged wilderness. The recent attacks carried out by the still-unknown band of insurgents had sent shockwaves through the control and command structure in Kamloops. To date, the campaign had uncovered a family of five who'd been barely getting by on a diet of roots, berries, nuts, fish and wild game. Fearing for the safety of their children, the parents surrendered as soon as their ramshackle cabin was surrounded by an NAP strike team.

Major Toombs knew that many more were in hiding. Just as the Thompson-Nicola District was beginning to experience its first guerrilla attacks, the fighting was growing fiercer in parts of Washington State, Oregon, Idaho, Alberta and Saskatchewan. In just one week alone, over one hundred of his colleagues had met their deaths. The resistance were like a cancer that had to be eradicated before it festered and grew out of control. The long-serving, cruel-hearted army and paramilitary officer knew better than to underestimate these tough-as-nails Western Canadian good ole' boys. They were very similar to his freedom-loving, gun-toting kin in the South. The same kin that would certainly hang him as a traitor should be ever show his face back there again. Toombs sat in the back of a Blackhawk helicopter. The pilots had recently dropped off a strike team in a remote area not far from Pinantan Lake.

*****

Sergeant-Major Bill Remple led an eight-member strike team up a rock-strewn hillside. The non-commissioned NAP members, their faces obscured by black ski masks, gripped their MP5s, M4 carbines and Franchi SPAS-12 combat shotguns. All were a bit winded by the time they reached the crest of the hill. All of a sudden the strike team was alerted by the indistinct sound of dogs barking. Big, loud dogs that would pick up the scent of approaching intruders and give their masters a heads-up.

Their adrenaline pumping, the troopers double-timed it toward a cabin hidden deep within the woods. It was rustic in every sense of the word, like a hastily-built trapper's cabin of yore. Using hand signals, Remple directed his men to move stealthily around the perimeter of the trees surrounding the cabin. Two large Rottweilers barked loudly as they spotted the militarized cops.

The strike team's sniper, a corporal named Charles, his entire six foot frame clothed in a gillie suit, fell into a firing position roughly fifty yards away from the cabin. Without warning, a man with a bushy, unkempt beard rushed outside waving a .30-30 rifle. Charles breathed deeply as he peered through the scope of his Remington M24 rifle. A hornet buzzed around his body. He lay perfectly still but the insect persisted in his efforts to harangue him. Then the hornet stung the sniper in the leg.

"Ah!" he yelled in pain.

The wild-eyed woodsman aimed his rifle in the direction of the noise. He fired two shots, one of which struck Charles in the head.

"Fire!" Remple yelled.

The strike team members unleashed a torrent of lead into the man. His body jolted as it was enfiladed with bullets. In less than a few seconds, he looked like a bloodied piece of Swiss cheese.

"Move it out!" the commander barked.

Just as the strike team was getting ready to move toward the cabin, another man armed with an AK-47 starting shooting at them from an upstairs window. In the confusion, as the troopers scrambled to take cover, one of them was struck in the abdomen area. The voice of Major Toombs came through the radio attached to the lapel on Remple's bulletproof vest.

"Ground team, what is your situation? Over."

We're taking heavy fire!" Remple braced his nerves as a bullet struck a tree inches from his head.

Working in unison, the strike team strafed a hail of bullets into the upstairs window. The second shooter fell onto the ground. Their boots pounding the earth, the strike team members burst inside of the cabin only to find it empty.

Chapter 30

Even though it had cost the life of another NAP trooper, the
recent hunting expeditions were proof to Frank Carragher that
progress was being made. Major Toombs stood at half-attention in
his superior's office. The young sniper who had lost his life the day

before, Zack Charles, had only been twenty-four years old. Three years earlier, he had graduated from a police sciences program at a community college in Peoria, Illinois.

"Major, those two enemy combatants who were eliminated yesterday. Have you been able to identify them yet?"

"Yes Sir. Mike Rundle and Pete Grimshaw. They are from the district."

"I assume that they were on the list of missing individuals."

"That I can't answer Sir."

Carragher sat down in front of the Mac computer on top of his desk. He double-clicked a folder on the desktop titled 'Residents Unaccounted For'. Of the more than one hundred citizens still unaccounted for, at least twenty had been flagged as potential threats to national security.

"You know Major, it's really interesting perusing these files. There's one young lady on the list…just let me bring up her file." Carragher clicked on the file for Sarah Jane Pearce. Sarah Jane's smiling photo appeared on the screen. "There it is. Sarah Jane Pearce. Age twenty-five. Law student at Thompson University. Environmental and social justice activist. Arrested during an anti-pipeline protest near Prince George two years ago. Oh, I notice that her file has been flagged."

Carragher browsed some other files.

"Some of these individuals have extensive military experience."

"I wonder how many of them have hooked up with Jake Scribner yet."

"Oh for Heaven's sake Major! Would you stop chasing that ghost? Put Scribner out of your mind. If I spent as much time worrying about that loser as you do, I'd get nothing done."

*****

For Brian Vance, spending long days in the burning desert sun guarding bridges or the Kamloops Airport was about as exciting as watching a pair of house flies mating. After the recent ambush that claimed the lives of three of their own, the Paras were on high alert. It pained Vance to see three of his fellow countrymen killed. This evening, as a flaming orange fireball of a sun signalled the close of another scorcher, Vance, Peter Huggins and two others members of the British Parachute Regiment, Harold Palmer and Mike Mooney, sat around the barracks playing cards and drinking beer. Cool air cranked out of an old air conditioner. There was very little to do in the city outside of their shifts.

On most days, it was boring. Vance yearned for the green, rolling hills of his homeland. He prayed that his time in Canada would not end being sent back to England in a coffin draped in the Union Jack. Although Vance generally got along with his fellow soldiers and even enjoyed good times with them, he was still a loner at heart. He found it hard to get into tonight's game.

"Hey Vance." Mooney took a puff of a cigar. "You playing with us or are you off in your own little world as usual?"

"Sorry." Vance turned back to his mates. "Guess my mind was wandering."

Palmer leaned in closer as if there was something major he had to tell his comrades but didn't want anybody else to hear.

"Looks like our answer to the lack of female affection has finally arrived," he said with a lewd smile.

"What do you mean Harold?" Vance asked.

"I'm not too sure if you blokes are aware of this or not, but a bunch of the guards over at the re-education centre have a small though lucrative business going on the side," Palmer said.

"I know about it," Vance stated. "They're trafficking innocent women and girls."

"That's a bit harsh but yes," Palmer replied. "And for a hundred Amero each, our needs will get taken care of."

"I'm all for that," Mooney said with a smile.

"Sign me up as well," Huggins added.

Vance was outraged at the way his mates were acting.

"How can you guys have anything to do with this? These so-called escorts are being coerced into doing this." Vance's comrades could feel the outrage in his voice.

"They're no good for anything else," Mooney said snidely. "Shit Brian, you wanting to be a virgin until you're forty? You gotta live a bit mate."

"I want no part of this." The young para's eyes were adamant. Set in stone.

"Figures." Mooney smiled mockingly at Vance. "Always had a feeling young Brian here was a fag."

Vance got up.

"Fuck you, Mooney."

This caused Mooney to get angry. Mooney, who was over six feet with broad shoulders and a barrelled chest, glowered over his smaller colleague.

"I'd love to see how tough you are you spoiled little wanker."

At that moment, Sergeant Allan Dowling entered the barracks.

"What the Hell is going on here?" The veteran paratrooper's voice was booming.

Mooney quickly distanced himself from Vance.

"Nothing Sergeant," Mooney said as Dowling glared at him with penetrating eyes.

Dowling looked upon Vance.

"Just a little disagreement Sergeant. We're all good here," Vance stated.

Not totally convinced that everything was fine, Dowling left the room. Mooney scowled menacingly at Vance.

"You better watch yourself there Vance. You turn against your mates, you've got nothing.

Chapter 31

The group members came to an agreement that it was simply too risky to stay where they had been for close to a month-and-a-half. Over the previous week, the guerrillas had been busy moving whatever provisions they had to their new location, the entire time constantly at risk of being spotted by the enemy. It was more than an hour north; an abandoned mine located between the Trans-Canada Highway and Wells Gray Provincial Park. Although the mine wasn't quite as cozy as the cabin had been, it was a much better location in the sense that it was very isolated. In addition, the interior of the mine, where the group would be living, was quite expansive.

The mine had two entrances; a small opening in the west-facing side of the mountain where an unknown mining company had closed the operation more than three decades earlier and a large entrance that would enable the freedom fighters to drive vehicles in and out. By now, each of them was quite familiar with almost every back road and trail that ran through their particular area of the vast wilderness. The evening before, Jake, Kevin, Sarah Jane, Mallory, Calvin and Neil had stored all of their food, ammunition and explosives on shelves in the cool dryness of the old gold mine. On a recent foraging expedition, Kevin and Calvin had found a working generator as well as an entire tank of fuel in an abandoned country estate. Having finished up a busy morning, they group sat around eating a lunch of canned soup and bread.

"I sure hope we can get that generator up and running," Calvin said. "This has been the first time in my life that I've had to live without electricity."

And you're surviving alright?" Jake said.

"Barely."

Neil finished up the remainder of the soup in his bowl.

"I wonder how old Shamus is doing. We ought to take a jaunt over to his place again soon," Neil stated.

"No, that'd be too risky," Jake said. "Unless this guy is completely off the radar, the authorities will most likely be monitoring him as well. We jeopardized our safety going there the first time."

At that moment, Sarah Jane and Mallory climbed down from the blanketed-off room they'd made for themselves on the loft. Both young women were carrying bags with shampoo and towels in them.

"Where are you ladies off to?" Jake asked.

"The lake," Sarah Jane replied. "God, it's been at least a week since any of us have washed."

"Alright!" Calvin exclaimed happily. "Neil and I will join you momentarily. We finally get to see you girls in the flesh."

"Not a chance in Hell!" Sarah shot back at him. She pointed at her breasts. "I wouldn't let you see these for all the money in the world."

*****

Not long after moving to their new home, the rebels, upon one of their hikes, had discovered a small lake half a kilometer or so away. The thin flip-flops Sarah Jane and Mallory wore on their feet provided scant protection from rocks that were strewn liberally amongst the narrow hiking trail. It was an amazingly bright and sunny afternoon. Hot but comfortably dry. By the time the two reached the shore of the lake, they were sweating. The sun caused the lake's shimmering blue waters to sparkle. The snow-capped peaks of nearby mountains were reflected in the lake. The entire scene was so tranquil and inviting.

"This is place is just beyond beautiful. It's a travesty that a war is going on all around us." Mallory had a hint of sadness in her voice.

"It pains my heart too, Mal. All we can do is just survive the best way we can."

Sarah Jane took off her flip-flops. She dipped the big toe of her left foot in the water. The chilly temperature caused her body to react.

"Is it cold?" Mallory asked.

"Freezing."

"It's a known fact that many of the lakes around here are glacier-fed," Mallory stated.

Sarah Jane and Mallory quickly took off their clothes until they were wearing just   bras and panties. Sarah Jane slowly entered the lake. Soon, she was up to her waist. Mallory, nervous, was hesitant to join her.

"Come on, Mallory."

"It's cold."

"It is at first. But once you're in, it only takes a minute or two to get used to it." Sarah Jane dunked her entire body in the lake. Seconds later, she emerged, shocked but invigorated. "Woah! That'll definitely wake you up after a long night of partying."

Mallory ever-so-slowly entered the water. The shock of the water hit her. Sarah Jane began soaping her body as her close friend made her way over.

"The lower half of my body is numb," Mallory said.

"You gotta dunk your head under."

Mallory took a deep breath.

"Okay, I'm going to do it." Mallory forced herself to go under. "That's so cold!" she shrieked as she emerged.

"Here you are," Sarah Jane said as she handed the bottle of body wash to Mallory, who began rubbing it all over her.

"I wonder how Bobbi, Marcia and Arianna are doing," Sarah Jane said as she and Mallory floated on their backs.

"I haven't heard from any of them since the end of school. Hopefully they're safe. Arianne lives all the way out in Atlantic Canada. Saint John, New Brunswick, I think. Sarah Jane, imagine us years from now. Old women telling everyone what we did to help restore freedom in North America."

"I've already done my part," Sarah Jane replied. "For a while, I was basically a professional protestor," she said with a laugh. "But I will not use violence to achieve my goals. Violence is something that stands against everything I believe in."

Chapter 32

Being separated from her mother was crushing Arielle. By now, she had made friends with all of the other kids locked up in the unit of the former correctional facility. Each day, the detainees were forced to listen to propaganda regarding how wonderful the Republic of North America was. It especially pained Arielle and indeed every child in there to be told repeatedly that their parents were traitors and enemies of the state. Arielle was constantly plagued by nightmares about that traumatic day when the masked gunmen burst into their home and forced them outside at gunpoint.

The children of the unit had just finished eating breakfast. It was time to prepare for the first class of the day. As the children filed into a classroom and took their seats, Ron Storey stood at the front of the room. Being in Storey's presence caused Arielle to shudder. He was every bit as loathed by the children as he was the adult political prisoners.

"Good morning. I firmly believe that you are finally starting to make progress." His scary eyes narrowed as they scanned the timid faces in front of him. "Some of you, at least. The rest stubbornly cling to the outlandish notion that life will magically return to the way it once was."

Storey pulled down a slide showing the North American flag. It followed another side of President Asher as well as the massive federal building in Denver that was the seat of the new republic's government.

"As far as any of you are concerned, President Asher is your father. There is no God, only the state."

Becky, a cute-freckled twelve-year-old girl, raised her hand. Becky's parents had been sent to a labor camp near the B.C.-Idaho border. She had been raised in a Baptist home.

"It says in the Bible that as Christians, we cannot serve two masters, meaning God and Man."

Irate, Storey glared upon her.

"I couldn't care less about what the Bible says." Becky drew back as he came aboard her. "Religion is superstitious and dangerous. And it has been outlawed by the North American government. Now I don't want to hear any more of that talk. If it continues, I will order you locked up in isolation."

Storey turned his attention back to his unwilling audience.

"There is no magical man in the sky who is going to swoop down and save all of you. Only by being good citizens and purging your minds of seditious thoughts can you be free again."

"You keep trying to scare us but it isn't going to work," Arielle uttered, a glint of defiance in her eyes.

Storey got right in her face.

"You're exactly the same as your mother," the commandant said." Insubordinate. Always insisting on pushing the envelope and believing you can get away with it. If you do not start conforming, you will stay here and that bitch mother of yours will be shipped to a labor camp either in the mountains or up north. Life is brutal in there. She will be forced to work sixteen hour days in often freezing or roasting hot conditions. And that's the last you will ever hear of her."

Arielle kept up a tough façade despite two single teardrops that seeped out of her eyes. It was plain as day that she had inherited her mother's side of the family's streak of stubbornness, of never backing down or giving up.

"Miss Clare, this is your last warning." Storey spoke in a somber tone. "One more outburst and you will be sent to solitary confinement indefinitely."

*****

Nicole yearned every bit as much to be with her only child. It was monotonous and depressing spending each day locked up like a dangerous criminal. The only thing that kept her going strong was the relationship she had developed with Bridgette. During the long hours that they were in their cell together, the two women talked, often sharing intimate details of their lives. They had even prayed together a few times.

A sense of dread and trepidation swept the female prisoners, particularly the younger, very attractive ones. Ron Storey and a group of high-ranking correctional officers, including Janet Paynter, were running a lucrative racket that included, almost always through coercion, compelling those young prisoners to sleep with North American Police officials, UN soldiers as well as high-ranking federal government officials who were posted in the city.

The illegal operation netted Storey and his cohorts generous sums of cash. Nicole, although older than many of the girls that had been selected was quite attractive herself. She too was concerned about the prospect of being forced to do such a revolting thing.

Nicole, Bridgette and another woman named Karen were getting tired from mopping up an entire corridor of the facility. Nicole resented having to do what amounted to little more than slave labor. The three women took little notice of Officer Stanford as he leaned against a wall supervising them. Compared to almost all of the other officers that worked in the facility, Stanford was friendly.

"That priest who came to visit you a couple of weeks ago. Is his name Father Tuck?" Bridgette asked.

"Yes," Nicole nodded.

"I believe my husband spoke to him on a couple of different occasions. Probably at the ecumenical meetings that used to be held at the university. I believe he operates a side business keeping bees and selling honey."

"He does from his home."

"Ladies, less talking and more working," Stanford said in a polite tone of voice.

Nicole winked at Bridgette as she focused on her work.

"You and I will have a chat later."

Chapter 33

Officials from the British Armed Forces Incident Investigation Team, based in Calgary, had concluded their investigation into the ambush three weeks earlier that claimed the lives of three members of the British Parachute Regiment. Lieutenant-Colonel Mullen had participated in the enquiry. It was a rare occasion when Mullen found himself eating lunch with Dan Toombs. The veteran British Army officer had developed a strong professional relationship with his North American Police counterpart. Although Mullen respected Toombs, quite often he was turned off by the Alabaman's self-aggrandizing attitude.

Toombs had a noticeable cruel streak in him as well. Borderline psychopathic. It was the same severe lack of conscience that had enabled Waffen SS officers and troops in Nazi Germany to commit horrific crimes against humanity many were later sent to the scaffold for. Although Mullen was first and foremost a soldier who never questioned orders, he also considered himself a humanitarian who wanted to help others. But as of right now, Mullen and Toombs had one thing in common; tracking down and annihilating those responsible for killing their subordinates.

"Anything new and exciting happening Major?" Mullen asked as he ate a garden salad.

"Business as usual."

"I spoke to Colonel Moresby this morning. He's with the army's Incident Investigation Team in Calgary."

"Yes, I've heard of it," Toombs stated.

"That improvised explosive device planted along the shoulder of the Trans-Canada Highway consisted of a pipe bomb taped securely to a propane cylinder. There was a timer attached to the pipe bomb."

"Just like years ago back in Iraq and Afghanistan." Toombs remembered his missions overseas.

"We sent out three helicopters and several drones to search for those rogues." Mullen's voice was rife with anger. "It almost seems like a lost cause. Peculiar that with a total gun ban in place, there would still be this heavy a volume of private firearms circulating around."

"Colonel, there's one thing I've learned since getting posted in the Great White North. If Canadians are anything, they're not like-and please, don't be offended by me saying this-your socialist European brethren who forfeited their rights decades ago. Believe me when I say that I had no shortage of misconceptions about this country as well as the people in it. And as much as I hate to admit it, Canadians are closer to being like Americans than you could ever imagine. They've resisted draconian gun laws, even outright confiscation. When those gun bans came into effect, tens of thousands of firearms simply 'disappeared' off the radar if you get my drift."

Chapter 34

Three half-melted pieces of ice floating at the surface of the glass of whisky in Frank Carragher's hand clinked together as he took a sip. From the balcony of his home, the lights of downtown Kamloops glittered in the hazy night. A housecoat covered his hairy, fat frame. He'd just taken a Jacuzzi bath with…what was her name again? Not that it mattered. The skinny brunette he was enjoying himself with was merely a commodity to be bought and sold. Carragher stepped back into the master bedroom.

There she lay-no older than twenty-two-listlessly on the king-sized bed. Although Carragher had found her charming, the feeling was far from mutual. What the career bureaucrat lacked in charm, he more than made up for with the sheer amount of power he wielded over every living creature in the nearly 46,000-square kilometer region. In the district administrator's day-to-day dealings with people, he couldn't help but exude the urban central Canadian elitist mindset that had been engrained into him from day one. He'd been educated in an expensive preppy private school in the Montreal suburb of Westmount. He had never known anything except for privilege.

Craving the sex he'd had great difficulty acquiring before, Carragher ordered those NAP troopers who were his personal bodyguards to bring women-particularly those of the young persuasion-to him. Most of these 'enemies of the state' had loved ones living in the district. Those who fulfilled his desires were granted special privileges. The young woman, whose name was Makayla, averted her eyes as Carragher sat down on the bed.

"You really made my night, ah… Makayla, isn't it?"

She nodded.

You don't have to be frightened of me. I'm generally a very reasonable as well as friendly person. But I have always been a strong believer in the honor system. Do what I tell you to do and you will be rewarded. Just out of curiosity, what offense have you been incarcerated for?"

"I wrote letters to local newspapers."

"What were they in regards to?"

"How big corporations have bought democratically elected governments and enslaved the citizens of Canada. Last time I checked, there was still freedom of speech in this country."

"Exactly what country are you referring to? Canada? Hasn't been freedom here in decades. The good ole' USofA? Definitely not Mexico or any one of the countless third world banana republics that were annexed into the union. There is only the Republic of North America. And have no illusions. The only rights you, I or any one of the five hundred million citizens of this nation have are the ones bestowed upon us by the government. I hope you do understand."

Makayla mildly resisted Carragher's advances as he moved closer to her.

"The good thing is, as of right now, you have been given a chance to redeem yourself-so to speak. Your crimes can be forgiven, but first you must completely renounce your old ways."

Doing an incredibly bad job of acting sexy, Carragher, silk thong underwear underneath his expansive waistline, lay down so he was face-to-face with Makayla. It was obvious even to him that she was turned off. She recoiled uncomfortably as he began accosting her.

"What's wrong? You didn't have any problem with me an hour ago."

"Please," she pleaded. "No more."

Makayla could sense the angry vibes emanating off of the autocratic leader.

"It isn't as though you have a tremendous amount of choice in the matter," He said. "Hell, you've got no choice but to do what you're told. Makayla, you don't seem to grasp what I am truly capable of doing. I can be your best friend or your worst enemy."

Makayla stirred unnervingly. She felt violated. Sickened at even being in the presence of this overweight, manipulative tyrant.

"Now if I'm not mistaken, your brother and his wife live here in the city. They haven't gone anywhere because they are prohibited from doing so. If you pleasure me, I will arrange for your brother to visit you. I might even get a few strings pulled so that you can have nicer accommodations inside of the facility. You do want freedom, don't you?"

Makayla's eyes began to tear up. She was caught between a rock and a hard place. This fiendish subhuman held her life in his hands. She thought of her older brother, Matthew, whom she hadn't seen since being locked up. Makayla put her loathing for Frank Carragher out of her mind and smiled seductively at him. It was an obvious façade but at least she was willing to do it, and that's all that mattered to him.

"Alright," Makayla said as she kissed Carragher. "I'm going to make you feel happier than you've ever felt in your entire life."

Chapter 35

It had taken quite a long time for all of the members of the guerrilla band to finally get along. Calvin and Sarah Jane were much more cordial to each other. Both had changed dramatically over the past few months. In order to be successful, each member of the group had to put their differences aside and work together.

It was a somewhat cooler day in the mountains. While Kevin had been wracking his brains since the morning trying to get the generator started, Sarah Jane and Mallory were out collecting berries, nuts and pine cones. Calvin and Neil were looking forward to the upcoming hunting season in September. Not that the old bureaucratic regulations applied anymore, but the best hunting took place in the fall of the year.

Jake's chiseled arms throbbed from spending over an hour splitting large blocks of firewood. He was sweating and getting tired. Jake didn't notice Sarah Jane approaching him. Although the environmentalist and social justice warrior had every intention of clinging to her belief system, a recent discussion with Mallory had made her question some very important things.

"Jake?"

Jake, his shirtless upper torso displaying a ripped physique, drove the head of the axe into a huge block of wood. Sarah Jane offered him a bottle of water, which he eagerly gulped down.

"Thanks Sarah."

"Jake, I've been questioning some things lately. You may find it strange hearing this from me, but I believe that it's time for me to learn how to shoot."

Jake smiled.

"Why the sudden change of heart?"

"Mallory and I had a discussion. I hate to admit it but you guys have been right all along. Peaceful protests and writing letters isn't going to cut it this time. Not that I have any desire to kill anybody. Just in case I have to protect myself."

Jake put his shirt back on. "If you're serious about learning, I have no problem teaching you. Come on inside for a minute."

Sarah Jane followed Jake inside of the mine. A steady electric hum signalled that the generator was finally up and running.

"You finally got it to work," Jake said.

Kevin sighed deeply, wiped sweat from his forehead. "It goddamn well took long enough," Kevin said tiredly.

"We need to borrow the AR."

"What for?"

"I'm going to give Sarah Jane some basic marksmanship lessons."

"That's great. The only thing is, we have to preserve as much ammo as possible."

"It's a good rifle to start on. We still have quite a few bullets for the British rifles," Jake stated. "We're only going to use twenty rounds."

"In that case, I guess it wouldn't be a problem. You're going to the rock quarry?"

"That's right. We need to take one of the ATVs."

*****

A rock quarry was located a quarter of a kilometer away from the mine. Inside of a rickety metal trailer was an old table and chairs. The rebels had set up the table and chairs a hundred yards from a huge mountain of gravel. Sarah Jane sat at the table. Jake could sense how nervous she was as he placed the AR-15 on the table.

"It's all fairly straightforward." Jake pointed to the dial on the side of the rifle and demonstrated the features. "Move it this way you have semiautomatic. This way it's on safety."

"So does this rifle shoot like thirty rounds a minute like those British assault weapons?"

"No, this rifle isn't fully automatic, just semi." Jake pointed at the button located an inch or so above the rifle's magazine and pressed it. A magazine fell out which he caught with his other hand. "That's the magazine release."

Sarah Jane pressed the butt of the AR-15 firmly against her shoulder.

"Now focus through the scope. Don't worry about parallax error as I've sighted in the scope exactly where it should be."

Sarah Jane took a couple of deep breaths before focusing on one of the two targets propped up in front of the mountain of gravel. She squeezed the trigger. The round missed the target by a few inches. She fired again. Same result. Frustrated, Sarah Jane lowered the AR-15.

"This is harder than it looks," Sarah Jane said with a chuckle.

"Just keep going. You'll get it."

Sarah Jane focused through the scope.

"I'll give you the same advice I gave Mallory. Aim about an inch or so below the target."

Sarah Jane, a little less nervous than she'd been, aimed just below the metal silhouette on the right side. She fired another round. It nicked the target. She fired again. This time, the bullet hit the target dead-centre. The sound of a bullet travelling at 2,700 feet-per-second slamming against heavy steel resounded through the air with a loud crrrack.

"Excellent work," Jake said. "Keep going the way that you are."

Chapter 36

The demonstrations became larger and more vociferous with each passing day. City residents, fully aware that their public displays of defiance were highly illegal, disregarded the district government as they marched in the streets of Kamloops and gathered daily in front of the former provincial correctional centre. Frank Carragher, despite being told constantly by his advisors to put a quick halt to the growing rebelliousness in the city, up until now had permitted the peaceful assemblies as a way of 'building a strong rapport with the plebes.'

It was mid-July and the Pacific Northwest was suffering through one of the hottest and driest summers on record. As food become scarcer in the district, more citizens, knowing they had absolutely nothing to lose, joined the burgeoning chorus of discontent. Due to late or missing shipments of food and other essential supplies, each time people entered local grocery stores, there were fewer and fewer items in the shelves.

All farms in the Thompson-Nicola District had been placed under the control of the Ministry of Agriculture, a completely unaccountable federal agency with Gestapo-like powers. Under the pain of severe punishment, producers were extra cautious not to break any of the thousands of tiny regulations regarding what they were allowed to grow and sell. Rationing had been put into effect. To date, there had been two massive rallies in the city decrying the actions of a government that was increasingly becoming hated by all.

Frank Carragher stood in the large window of the Jim Canfield Building. Major Toombs stood beside him. On the street below, hundreds of city residents gathered in front of the large government office building. They waited to hear a group of local activists who had set up a podium near the steps of the Jim Canfield Building.

As the rally was getting underway, Robert Hunt and Marty Smith were walking down nearby Victoria Street. The charismatic-looking young man in his late twenties standing behind the podium with another man and two young women didn't appear familiar. Steven Fenton was a popular social activist, writer and radio talk show host. The demonstrators mobilized in front of Fenton were a mixture of older residents, men, women and children. Many of them carried signs bearing slogans such as 'Restore Civil Liberties', 'Canada is not the 51st State,' 'Canada is not for sale' and 'Destroy the New World Order.'

Toombs glanced over at his supervisor, who appeared to be deep in thought.

"Sir, they've pushed their luck to the limit. You give citizens an inch and they take a country mile."

"This Steven Fenton character. What do you know about him, Major?"

"Not a great amount, Sir. I believe he's from Vancouver. Amazing how he slipped under our radar."

"We'll just watch and see how this event goes. This hooligan has troublemaker written all over him."

On the street below, all eyes were focused on Fenton as he placed his mouth to the microphone.

"Good afternoon my friends and neighbors! This is the people's mic!"

"This is the people's mic!" the crowd responded with fervor.

"Like all of you, I am sick and tired of seeing foreign military forces and corporations as well as our own traitorous Canadian government stripping us of our civil liberties, locking up our family members and friends and starving us into submission." Fenton spoke with fiery passion. "To add insult to injury, these same traitors are sending our young Canadian men and women overseas to fight never-ending wars. All of this is being done in the name of a bloody, greed-stricken corporate agenda that serves no one except for the global elites and their cronies in the military industrial complex."

Hunt and Smith were quite impressed by Fenton's speech. The freedom fighters, who planned to stir up some mayhem themselves in the very near future, made sure that they were far enough away from the crowd should the goon squad arrive.

"People," Fenton continued. "The time has come to send a message to our overlords in Denver that we will no longer tolerate being treated like serfs by this illegal regime. Turncoats in both nations have sold out the good citizens of Canada and the United States. As Canadians, it is our duty to protect our sovereignty and our natural resources."

Frank Carragher's eyes become more sinister-looking as Fenton's speech intensified. He turned to Toombs.

"I'm ordering you to drop the hammer, Major. You've just been given the power to crush every one of those dissident aggressors."

"I'm looking forward to it, Sir," Toombs replied with an evil grin. He took a cellular phone out of his pocket and dialled a number. "Captain, send in the tactical force."

Fenton took a sip of water before continuing his speech.

"We, the citizens of the Thompson-Nicola District, demand the release of all political prisoners."

Fenton looked out into the crowd. A young woman jumped up and raised her hand to get his attention.

"You there," Fenton said with a smile as he pointed at her. "Would you like to say something?"

The woman, who was in her early thirties, rushed up to the podium.

"What is your name? Speak into the mic. Tell everyone who you are."

"Nancy Richards," she announced to the crowd. "I have three children. My husband is dead. We haven't eaten in two days. We continue to suffer while those pieces of shit in this building live high on the hog. Well, I say no more. It has to stop."

At that moment, a column numbering over one hundred NAP troopers marched in lockstep in a v-shaped formation down the street towards the crowd. They were all garbed head-to-toe in thick black Kevlar body armor. Helmets with visors protected their faces. As they marched, the troopers hit their truncheons against thick Plexiglass shields. The demonstrators looked on in fear and apprehension as a couple of the riot squad troopers raised tear gas launchers and guns. In less than a minute, the crowd found itself overwhelmed by tear gas. People stumbled about coughing, wheezing and disoriented. Terrified children separated from their parents cried.

The militarized riot police fired a volley of rubber bullets into the quickly dispersing crowd. Several of the demonstrators reeled in horrendous pain as they were hit by the projectiles. Next, the troopers rushed headlong into the crowd. The demonstrators did their best to protect themselves from the blows the troopers mercilessly unleashed on them.

Marty Smith felt his adrenaline rising as he watched his fellow Kamloops residents being beaten and hauled away by NAP troopers. He went to go but Bob Hunt held him back.

"No Marty. Not here. Not now."

"God sake Bob. We have to do something!"

"Don't worry. Every one of those fascist goons is getitng what's coming to them. Karma is a real bitch sometimes," Hunt said. "But we cannot get involved now. Let's just discreetly walk away before they see us."

*****

Nicole's head hurt from sitting through three hours straight of mindless propaganda classes that were designed to completely brainwash and social engineer the political prisoners. A few of Nicole's fellow detainees had begun to crack under the daily stress. Nicole made a vow to herself that she could never be worn down physically or mentally. In her heart, she longed to be free and that burning desire would never be extinguished.

Nicole had been informed that she had a visitor. It could only be one individual and she knew it. To ensure that the guards would not suspect she was harboring ulterior thoughts, Nicole played along each day, asking questions and participating in the re-education classes.

Nicole even pretended that she was in full agreement with the lies and deception spewed forth out of the mouths of the guards and government officials from the Ministry of Information.

As Nicole was escorted into one of the small interrogation rooms she'd been in umpteen times before, it was a contenting sight to see Father Julian Tuck sitting there.

"Hello Nicole. I just finished up my rounds counselling some of the other detainees. Lieutenant Paynter permitted me to meet with you but only briefly. I apologize for not being in to see you as frequently as I'd like. My life is busier now than it's ever been. You're holding up okay?"

"As best I can under the circumstances," Nicole replied unemotionally. "I'm still unsure when I will be allowed to see Arielle."

"You're not the only one who's been wondering about that. I've spoken personally with Captain Storey. If I didn't know better, I'd say he has a vendetta against you."

"Me and many others."

Just then, the door opened. Janet Paynter appeared. "Alright, time's up."

Tuck smiled politely and slowly stood up.

"We will talk again very soon Nicole," Tuck said. "I promise you that."

Chapter 37

The previous day's events continued to weigh heavily on Frank Carragher's consistently overloaded mind. Although the ringleaders as well as several demonstrators had been arrested and were currently being held in detention, the district administrator feared that these outward displays of defiance were proof that the cracks in the proverbial dam were getting larger. With the combined strength of NAP and UN forces unable to eradicate the mounting insurgency just a few hours south of him, Carragher was beginning to believe that it would only be a matter of time before he too was faced with the same situation.

Although the heavy-handed bureaucrat's sexual needs were being adequately being taken care of, he yearned for something better. His staff continued to bring him young women, some barely of legal age. Sure, Carragher enjoyed their company, but what he truly desired was an older, mature woman, perhaps in the neighborhood of thirty-five to forty-two. Major Toombs entered his superior's spacious office with two NAP troopers. Carragher was preoccupied peering through the files of several of the women who were detained in the re-education facility. He himself had not yet been inside of there. After studying the profiles, the district administrator set his eyes upon a local country girl with a warm demeanor and infectious smile.

'Nicole Clare. Age thirty-five. Chemical researcher, freelance journalist and blogger. One daughter, Arielle, age seven.'

"Interesting," Carragher said as he perused Nicole's profile. He looked up at Toombs.

"Good afternoon, Major."

"Good afternoon, Sir. You will be most pleased to learn that Steven Fenton, Laura Winwood, Rachel Beckerman and Peter Krowlikowski have all been sentenced to indefinite forced labor. The latter are Fenton's compatriots."

"Yes, I'm aware of that. Major Toombs, there is something I need you to do for me."

"I will do my best to fulfill your command."

"Come over here for a minute."

The troopers stood at attention as Toombs walked over behind Carragher's desk. On the computer was a photo of Nicole Clare.

"Major, I would like you to arrange for me to have an audience with this woman. She appears much more mature than the others. Very attractive too I must add."

Toombs appeared hesitant.

"Is there a problem?"

"Sir, with all due respect, what I am about to tell you is both shocking and true. Nicole Clare is the fiancé of Jake Scribner."

"You just won't let that die, will you?" Carragher said.

"Sir, please, hear me out. This woman, a blatant enemy of the state, has publicly denounced the federal government, President Asher and just about everybody else you could imagine. She is dangerous and cannot be trusted."

"Well, according to Ms. Clare's file, she's been a good girl since arriving at the facility. There have been no flare-ups. She attends daily classes without question. Does exactly as she's told."

"Sir, her daughter is locked up in there as well."

"I know that Major."

"She's just going through the motions."

Carragher looked up at his right-hand man.

"Would you be willing to bet your lavish, gold-plated pension on that, Major Toombs? I've never been one to pass judgment too quickly. If Ms. Clare is indeed joined to Scribner the way you claim that she is, then we can most certainly use that to our advantage. Like every other prisoner in that place, she's in a desperate situation. And desperate people do what they have to in order to survive."

"Sir, I just wish you'd reconsider---"

"I will hear no more of your negatively, Major Toombs. I always get what I want and right now I want her. I gave you an order. I expect it to be carried out. Dismissed."

Toombs half-saluted Carragher.
"Yes, Sir."
He then walked out of the office.

Chapter 38

Robert Hunt fidgeted nervously as he watched the front door of the house. The retired Mountie understood that he was taking an enormous risk simply by hosting this illegal gathering. He knew these men quite well. There was almost zero chance that any of them could be informers. Still, one had to keep his guard up. Ding. Ding. Ding. Three rings of the traditional doorbell chime. Hunt got up from the recliner in the living room and opened up the door. Marty Smith, along with Jeff Hinton and his son Benjamin as well as an incredibly-built early thirtyish man named Chris Templeton, were outside. Hunt had never met Templeton before. Jeff Hinton was in his early fifties. He worked as a computer technician. Benjamin was in his early twenties.

"Good evening Bob," Hinton said. He could sense his friend's uneasiness.

"Hi Jeff. Marty. Ben. You must be Chris Templeton."

"Yes," Templeton replied quietly.

"Well come on in then."

The visitors entered. Hunt checked his watch. 7:30 p.m. Curfew came into effect at 11:00 p.m. sharp.

Hunt and Templeton shook hands.

"It's great to meet you," Hunt said to the broad-shouldered, muscle-bound man. "Marty tells me you were in the Canadian Army."

"I was in for ten years. Special Operations group," Templeton explained. "I got out just before the world war started although I was involved in some NATO missions in Eastern Europe."

"We need a man with your skill set on board this mission," Hunt told him.

There was a rapt knock at the door. Hunt opened it. Father Tuck was standing on the doorstep. He was dressed in a light jacket, cotton pants and sneakers. Jeff Hinton and Marty Smith looked to Hunt as if wondering 'what is he doing here?'

"Good evening, Father. Let me take your jacket."

Tuck removed his jacket, which Hunt hung up on a hook.

"Let's go down to the basement fellas," he said.

The six men descended the stairs into the basement. As Benjamin, Tuck and Templeton sat down on couches in the rec room, Hinton and Smith took Hunt aside.

"Bob, why is that priest here?" Smith asked. "Look, although I have no use whatsoever for organized religion, I have nothing against your faith or anybody else's. But considering that he's a clergyman, and most have disappeared from the city, there's a strong probability he's working for the government."

"Yeah," Hinton added. "You've potentially jeopardized this entire operation just by telling him about it."

"Now just hold on a minute here, guys," Hunt shot back. "In case you're not aware, Father Tuck knows more about what's going on than we do. He's at the former provincial jail at least three days a week. He's more or less the de facto chaplain there."

Smith calmed himself down.

"We just can't take any chances. That's all I'm saying Bob."

"Don't worry. We're not. Now let's get this meeting started," Hunt stated.

Everyone sat down except for Hunt.

"Gentlemen, the time has come for us to reclaim our city. This is our land for crying out loud! Now while it's true that these occupying forces may have the capability to control the perimeter of the city, they cannot watch every one of us twenty-four seven. And we are about to become a real thorn in their side."

Benjamin half-raised his hand.

"We need to cut off the head of the snake," Benjamin proclaimed. "That piece of shit control freak Carragher. I know exactly where he lives too."

Hinton turned to his son.

"That's too risky, Ben."

"It is too risky," Hunt continued. "Carragher's home would be under round-the-clock surveillance. Another reality we have to keep in mind is that once we start launching our attacks, the local authorities will most likely retaliate against the population."

"We have to target some of the bigwigs," Smith stated. "If not Carragher, then how about that British colonel? Better yet, that sadistic thug Toombs. That animal shot Arnold Hooper after Arnold refused to allow a squad of those NAP goons to enter his home. Oh, believe me. I'll be the first to put a bullet in his brain."

Hunt lowered his voice.

"I won't say any names, but I have a man on the inside at the re-education facility. He's an acquaintance of mine. I assume you know who the commandant of that place is now."

"It's not Raymond Johnson, is it?" Hinton asked. "Oh no, he took early retirement."

"Ron Storey." The tone of Hunt's voice was sombre.

Just hearing that name infuriated Jeff Hinton.

"I remember when that power-tripping brute was in charge of the group of police and UN disarmament officers who went door-to-door seizing firearms. Thank God I had already buried mine in the ground. Soon as I can sneak out of town they're getting dug up."

"Storey is operating a sex trafficking ring out of the facility," Hunt stated.

"Come again." Templeton was shocked.

"Storey, along with a small group of officers, sells female prisoners to government officials as well as NAP and UN troops. Son of a bitch has been doing this for months. He lives close to downtown. My source tells me he often works late, sometimes past midnight."

"Bob, all of this sounds wonderful in theory, but looking at reality, how are we supposed to sneak around without getting caught?" Hinton asked. "Anybody caught out after curfew is guaranteed a one-way trip to the gulag."

"Or the grave," Templeton added. "We should be focusing on destroying basic infrastructure such as bridges, buildings, vehicles...whatever."

"We'll just have to work all of this out over the next week or so," Hunt stated. "In the interim, carry on as if nothing is happening. And whatever you do, do not let another living soul know what is going on. I cannot emphasize that enough."

Chapter 39

The scorching summer heat lagged on into August. For the past two days, Calvin and Neil had been travelling by ATV through the forest trails that ran parallel to the North Thompson River. The rebels were conducting reconnaissance missions. They monitored the volume of enemy activity that crossed the bridges over the river. Camouflaged in tan, black and green fatigues, the duo crouched down amongst the straggly bone-dry spruce and pine trees that dotted the hot, dry hills on either side of the North Thompson River. For the past few hours, Calvin and Neil had been watching the bridge outside of Barriere. From their position, the small community appeared very quiet. Three North American Police troopers stood guard on the bridge that spanned high above the fast-flowing river.

"Calvin, do you believe that this is a good candidate?"

"Most definitely. From the looks of things, this bridge is used frequently. Once we blow the bridge, it will take their engineers a considerable amount of time to rebuild it, possibly months."

"Anything to slow them down," Neil said. "We better be getting back to base. They're going to be wondering if something happened to us or not."

*****

Calvin and Neil returned to camp just as the others were making dinner. As the group ate, they listened to a broadcast on an old radio Kevin had managed to get hooked up. It was an illegal broadcast from the Underground Patriot Network, a clandestine news organization located somewhere in the American Southwest. The Unified Movement to Restore North America, a conglomeration of militias and guerrilla bands scattered throughout the continent, urged all citizens to fight back against the foreign and domestic military forces at every opportunity. Many of the insurgent units operated in the reclaimed areas of the continent such as western Texas, New Mexico, Oklahoma, Montana, Wyoming as well as parts of Alberta and Saskatchewan. How long these ragtag, isolated groups would be able to hold out against superior forces was another matter entirely.

"At least we're <u>slowly</u> inching our way towards victory," Mallory said quietly. There was a trace of hope in her voice.

"Unfortunately, not here," Jake said. "So far, it would appear that we are the only ones in this entire region of B.C. who are actively resisting. If the district doesn't erupt in rebellion-and soon-we may be up shit creek without a paddle."

Kevin had spent a considerable amount of time fiddling with one of the blasting caps Shamus O'Reilly had given to the rebels. It took an incredible amount of steady nerves, but he finally got the device to work.

"How hard will it be to sneak in there undetected, blow up that bridge and get out before all hell reigns down upon our heads?" Kevin asked his nephew.

"Because that is a frequent crossing area, there is a small contingent of NAP troopers who work on twelve-hour rotations," Calvin explained. "Usually two or three on during a shift."

The rebels munched on wild game they had caught a day earlier.

"We take out the sentries," Jake said. "Those night vision scope fit our rifles perfectly. Now, we'll have to carry out this attack late, at least at midnight. We have four blocks of C4. We're going to use two of them for this operation." Jake looked at Sarah Jane. "Are you ready yet?"

"I'll come along. Observe. But I flat-out refuse to---"

"We're well aware of your stance on war." Jake turned to Calvin and Mallory. "As it turns out, you two are the best snipers in the group. You will be in charge of popping the sentries. Kevin and I will set the charges."

"On what night are we going to do this Jake?" Neil asked.

"I'm thinking perhaps two days from now. We're probably going to end up spending a night or two in the woods so we'll have to bring some extra provisions along with us."

Chapter 40

The stress of being separated from Jake and Arielle was really starting to take its toll on Nicole. She'd lost fifteen pounds since late April. The monotony of daily life inside of the detention facility coupled with abusive treatment at the hands of guards was enough to cause even the toughest individual to break down mentally. Even Bridgette wasn't sure if she could hold out for much longer. She was desperate to see her husband and son again. Nicole and Bridgette joined eight other inmates in the showers. The hot water cascading over Nicole's body brought scant relief from all of the turmoil that was wracking her. Once they were finished, the close friends dried themselves off. Janet Paynter appeared in the locker room doorway. Her cold, unfeeling eyes were set upon Nicole.

"Clare, get dressed and come with me. You've got a visitor."

Nicole was a trifle nervous. Who would be wanting to see her at this time of the evening?" She touched Bridgette on the shoulder.

"I'll see you later, okay?"

"I'll be where I always am," Bridgette said with a weak smile.

Nicole felt anxious as she was escorted down the long corridor that led into the administrative area of the prison. A guard hit a button. The door separating Nicole and her guards slid open with a buzzing sound.

Captain Storey and another guard, a sergeant, smiled lewdly at Nicole as she was escorted into an office.

"You do exactly as the nice man says and you may just survive," Storey said to her.

Nicole replied with a deep, penetrating scowl. One of the guards opened the office door. Nicole entered. She was flabbergasted at the sight of Frank Carragher sitting there. He rose to greet the shocked inmate. Nicole knew very little about the plump administrator. He was about the only person she hadn't yet disparaged.

"Please, take a seat, Ms. Clare."

Nicole sat down in front of him.

"How are you doing?"

"Surviving. That's all most of us can do these days."

Carragher studied Nicole's face. It was devoid of emotion.

"I know a great deal about you. Nicole Clare, the famous local liberty blogger and activist."

"I'm curious as to the reason why you summoned me here."

"Your daughter resides in the children's area. Arielle."

Prompted by a rush of adrenaline, Nicole shot up from her chair.

"If you or anybody even thinks of doing anything to her…"

"Relax, Nicole. Nobody is hurting anybody. Now, from what I understand, you wish to be reunited with Arielle. Before you react, please hear what I have to say. I have a proposition for you. I assume you're aware that I hold complete dominion over each and every living creature that resides within the confines of this district. Anyway, I've had my share of women since arriving in this rather dull, smelly city. Young ones mainly. Didn't really do anything for me. Nicole, I must say, there is something about you that I find beyond attractive. Sexy. The kind of mature sexy that can only be acquired through years of experience. I think you know where I'm going with this."

"In your dreams."

Carragher smiled wickedly.

"Nicole, you obviously do not understand the ramifications of what you're doing by rejecting my most generous offer. You're being presented with the opportunity of a lifetime. Should you become my paramour, I will ensure that you have a much better life than what you have in this cesspool. You and Arielle will get to spend as much time together as possible. Eventually, you will be allowed to live in the community again. I seriously suggest that you put a lot of thought into this before deciding to reject it."

Chapter 41

The stillness of the pitch black night was interrupted only by the sound of the fast-flowing North Thompson River. Save for a handful of streetlights, the town of Barrierre was dark as well. The six guerillas stalked silently up a hill that afforded a clear view of the bridge that connected Yellowhead Highway 5. The bridge was three-hundred yards away. Jake peered through a pair of night-vision goggles. Three NAP troopers walked around on the bridge.

Jake nodded to Calvin and Mallory. Mallory, her hands grasping the Lee Enfield, got into a firing position. Calvin, holding the Nosler M48, did the same. Both rifles had homemade sound suppressors made from car oil filters which were screwed onto the ends of the barrels. Calvin breathed deeply before he focused his attention through the crosshairs of the night-vision scope on the Nosler. An NAP trooper was quite visible through the greenish-black color of the night-vision goggles. He pulled the trigger. The NAP trooper collapsed to the ground after being hit in the upper chest.

Mallory watched anxiously as the fallen trooper's comrades rushed to his aid. She focused the crosshairs on the head of one of them and fired. The bullet pierced an ugly hole in the man's forehead before he too went down. Before the third trooper could raise his rifle, Calvin took him out.

"Good job, guys," Jake said with a smile before turning to Kevin. "Clock's a tickin' my friend."

Kevin held up two bricks of C4, both of which had blasting caps embedded in them.

"Hopefully it takes a while for reinforcements to arrive," he stated.

Jake turned to Calvin, Neil, Mallory and Sarah Jane.

"Monitor the east side of the bridge very closely. If there are only a few more troopers posted in the town, we should be able to get them. Actually Neil, I'm going to get you to help us toss those bodies off of the bridge."

"Sure," the young aboriginal-Canadian replied.

Jake, Kevin and Neil made their way to the bridge. Jake and Kevin had British rifles slung over their shoulders. The bridge was very well-lit, possibly enough for them to get spotted. Jake felt his heart racing. He sweated nervously. One by one, the three rebels picked up the slain troopers and tossed them into the North Thompson far below. Neil eyed their MP5s.

"We should take their weapons," he said in almost a whisper.

"After we get this done," Kevin replied. "Jake, I'm thinking the best place to plant the C4 is on the girders."

"How do you plan on getting underneath to put them into place?"

"That isn't necessary," Kevin replied. "Lots of places right along the deck."

Kevin kneeled down near the side of the bridge deck. Along the stiffening girder were several small slots. He placed a brick of C4 into one of them. Then he went over to the other side of the bridge. Kevin placed the remaining brick of the highly-malleable plastic explosive in one of the slots in the stiffening girder.

"Mission accomplished," the ex-combat engineer said.

"Glad we were able to pull this off without a hitch," Jake said.

The three guerrillas quickly made their way off of the bridge. They walked through the rough terrain to where Calvin, Mallory and Sarah Jane waited.

"I assume it went well," Sarah Jane stated.

"Perfect," Kevin replied.

Kevin removed two detonators from the pockets of his camouflage jacket. The others braced themselves as Kevin pressed a small button on each of the detonators. Seconds later, two ear-shattering explosions rocked the ground under their feet. Sarah Jane and Mallory looked on in shock as the bridge deck, followed by the girders, started to come loose. In no time at all, the middle entire of the bridge gave way and plummeted into the dark waters far below. It was an awesome yet nerve-jangling sight. The rebels retreated west toward the forest road over a kilometer away where the Ford Explorer was parked.

Chapter 42

A pressing tension enfiladed the small group of would-be rebels that were gathered in the basement of Bob Hunt's home. The group was having a short briefing before heading out into the night to wreak as much havoc as they could. It was already 8:30 p.m. The city was generally quiet at this time of the evening save for a few citizens walking around as well as the odd armored NAP patrol. Hunt produced a Sig Sauer handgun, on the end of which was a sound suppressor.

"Bob, where in hell were you able to get that?" Jeff Hinton asked.

"I'm a retired police officer. I can acquire damn near anything. Now, as I was saying…"

Benjamin half-raised his hand.

"That priest who was here the other night. Where is he now?"

"Yeah," Jeff chimed in. "You said he was helping us."

"Oh, don't worry, Tuck is every bit a part of this group as you all are. That seemingly quiet man has access to most of the big government buildings around Kamloops. You may find it hard to believe, but there are still many folks in our society who trust priests and ministers, including NAP officers and those foreign soldiers who've been terrorizing our city. That is why Tuck is such an integral part of this team."

Though nervous, Hunt felt quite confident about what he was about to do.

"As I was trying to say," Hunt continued. "Jeff, Ben and myself will take out the first target. Chris, you've done some recon on that house in the West End, have you not?"

"I certainly have," Templeton replied. "From what I can gather, many of the homes in the vicinity of that old Victorian-style house are empty. That means no innocent civilians living in them. Four high-ranking members of the North American Police are living there. To the best of my knowledge, there is a lieutenant, a sergeant-major and maybe two staff sergeants."

"You say you have gelignite?" Hunt asked.

"A small amount that I acquired from an individual who will remain unnamed," Templeton stated.

*****

Ron Storey lived by himself in a small bungalow in a neighborhood a short ten-minute drive from downtown Kamloops. The veteran law enforcement officer and prison warder had been married once, over ten years earlier. Storey's ex-wife accused him of being controlling and verbally abusive, allegations he flatly denied. Although the night was dark, stars filled the sky. Storey was beat tired from the twelve-hour shift he'd just logged at the former provincial jail. He pulled his three-year-old Prius into the driveway of his home. He'd have just enough energy for a glass of bourbon and then it was right off to bed. Storey got out of the Prius, locked it and moved toward the house.

Hunt, Jeff and Ben Hinton lurked in the thick vegetation of a hedge that separated Storey's home from his neighbor's. Ensuring that nobody could be watching them, the three insurgents, their faces concealed by black balaclavas, moved slowly out of the hedge. Ben Hinton's heart pounded wildly as he watched Ron Storey walk up to the doorstep.

Storey fiddled with the umpteen keys that were attached to the ring of his driver's keys. He was tired, cranky and simply wanted to put another stressful day behind him. As Storey found the house key, he felt a slight movement. It was either around or directly behind him.

"What the Hell?"

Storey turned around. His body went numb with fear as an individual whose face was concealed by a ski mask pointed a Sig Sauer at him. Before Storey could get any words out, the intruder fired a muted shot point-blank between his eyes. Storey collapsed onto the doorstep. Hunt quickly retreated back toward the shrub where Jeff and Ben Hinton waited anxiously.

"We have to get out of here fast," Hunt stated as he breathed heavily.

As the trio removed their masks and sauntered out onto the boardwalk as if nothing had ever happened, Hunt discreetly dropped the Sig Sauer into a storm sewer. Further down the street, the three bicycles they'd used to get here were hidden in a small suburban park.

"If we get stopped for questioning," Hunt said, "We're simply out for a quick bike ride before curfew."

Chapter 43

It was an old neighborhood of picturesque Victorian-style homes, many of which were well in excess of 150 years old. Chris Templeton and Marty Smith had parked their car a couple of blocks away. The two walked casually up Granada Street as if they had been living in the upscale neighborhood their entire lives. Tucked securely inside Templeton's jacket was a stick of gelignite with a blasting cap embedded firmly into it. The particular house they were targeting was very stately with white siding, black shutters and had three floors. Templeton spotted the propane tank attached to the right side of the house.

The rebels approached with great caution. Smith could see the home's occupants-two men and two women. Their inebriated shouts and laughter could be heard beyond the confines of the dwelling. Templeton took out the gelignite. He placed it on top of the propane tank. Templeton nodded. They walked out onto the sidewalk and continued walking briskly down Granada Street. As soon as they were within striking distance of the car, Templeton removed a detonator from his jacket pocket. He pressed a button. Seconds later…kaboom! The immediate area was rocked by a thunderous explosion followed by an electrifying fireball that shot up into the night sky.

Templeton and Smith watched as they saw the results of their handiwork.

"Anybody for roasted pig?" Templeton asked with a wicked grin.

"Trying to cut pork out of my life," Smith replied. "We better get out of here quickly. Lo and behold, those jackbooted thugs will be interrogating everybody within a ten-kilometer radius of this place.

*****

Frank Carragher slept peacefully. The career bureaucrat had been sleeping much better lately. His dreams were filled with memories of faraway places that he'd visited or longed to visit. All of a sudden, Carragher's serene, subconscious imaginings were abruptly ended by the annoying buzzing of his cellular phone, which vibrated wildly on the night table beside his bed. Astounded as to why his phone was ringing this late into the evening, Carragher groggily reached over to get it.

"If this isn't a matter of life or death…"

"Sir, my apologies." Major Toombs was on the other end. "There's been an explosion…on Granada Street in the West End."

Carragher shot up.

"A bombing?" The district administrator was shocked.

"Certainly looks that way Sir. Four members of the NAP lived in that house. From the looks of things, none of them survived."

Chapter 44

A charred, smoking ruin was all that remained of the beautiful gentrified home. The propane tank was a hollow, burned-out metal shell. Members of the North American Police Special Investigation Unit sifted through the remains in a desperate search for clues. Other troopers had cordoned off the area. Armored units and helicopters spanned out across the city looking for yet-unidentified suspects.

Frank Carragher pulled up to the curb on the street in front of the home. Major Toombs and Lt. Colonel Mullen stood back watching the investigators ply their trade. Carragher was appalled at the sight.

"Major, any idea how they managed to blow up the house?"

"They attached some sort of explosive device to the propane tank outside," Toombs responded.

Carragher seethed angrily.

"I can only speculate as to who is to blame for this mass murder. I do find it incredibly hard to believe that somebody could simply sneak past the security perimeter surrounding Kamloops without being spotted, carry out this blatant act of terrorism and sneak out like the proverbial thief in the night."

"This isn't exactly a small town," Mullen said. "There are many residents, mainly ex-service personnel, who are capable of inflicting such damage."

Toombs glanced over at Carragher.

"Sir, perhaps now you will heed my advice. The amount of personnel both Colonel Mullen and I command in this district is simply not adequate enough to police it effectively. As you're well aware, a small, committed band of insurgents can be more of a threat than an entire professional army. The only way we are going to find these terrorists and instill enough fear into the hearts of the populace is by cordoning off the city neighborhood by neighborhood and going door-to-door. Search every single home top-to-bottom. Any resident found in the unlawful possession of any type of weapon will automatically forfeit his or her life."

"Public executions. Now there's an idea worth exploring," Carragher said. "Colonel Mullen, do you know a General Nilsson? He's with the United Nations base in Edmonton."

"Name rings a bell, Sir," Mullen said. "If you had any idea how many UN troops are stationed in North America…let's just say we're many."

"I had a Skype conversation with General Nilsson a couple of days ago. He is just waiting for the green light to send three hundred Norwegian peacekeepers to Kamloops. They are expected to arrive within the next day or so."

The three looked on in horror at the ghastly sight of four bodies being carried out of the house on stretchers. The bodies were scorched beyond recognition. Two had been half-carbonized.

Toombs and Mullen lowered their heads forlornly.

"I'd known Gerald Cairns for decades," Toombs said. "John Richardson had just been promoted to lieutenant. I didn't know the two women. One had spent twenty years in the RCMP. She was a staff sergeant."

At that moment, an NAP corporal who'd been talking on his radio put it away and approached Toombs.

"Sir, there's been another murder."

"Where at Corporal?" Toombs asked. "My God, this just keeps on getting better," he said sarcastically.

"All I know is that it happened in some neighborhood close to the downtown area."

"One of ours?" Toombs asked in horror.

"Not exactly, Sir. Victim's name is Ron Storey," the corporal affirmed.

"Isn't that the commandant of the re-education facility?" Mullen asked Toombs.

Toombs nodded as he cringed in anger. He shouted out to an NAP sergeant who was talking with a couple of the investigators.

"Sergeant Geraldton, we have to get down to that murder scene right away."

Geraldton walked over to him.

"No problem, Major. A couple of the special investigations guys are coming with us."

Chapter 45

The mysterious killing of one of the most despised men in the entire Thompson-Nicola District brought relief for many of the beleaguered detainees locked up inside the detention centre. The NAP searched every square inch of the area surrounding Ron Storey's home. The murder weapon had disappeared. No fingerprints had been found at the crime scene. Nicole took delight in the fact that some individual or group of individuals had had the courage to take out the demented, sadistic human trafficker. She, along with the other female inmates, was hopeful that Storey's death would bring an end to the regime of terror and abuse that had taken place under his watch. But then again, Janet Paynter was almost as depraved as he had been and she was next in line to become commandant.

Nicole and Bridgette stood in line in the facility's cafeteria. Nicole had barely slept a wink over the previous two nights. She had just been faced with the most difficult decision of her life. Barring a massive uprising, becoming Frank Carragher's sex slave was about the only way she would ever get to hold Arielle again, much less gain any freedom. Not a minute passed by where she didn't have Jake on her mind. Oh, to be in his rugged arms once again...she quickly snapped herself back to reality. Fantasizing about things she couldn't have-at least not right now-only made everything worse. The women found a place at the end of a long table.

"The Lord certainly works in mysterious ways," Bridgette stated as she sipped coffee.

"What do you mean?"

Nicole took a bite of the scrambled eggs on her plate. They tasted like rubber. Bridgette leaned in closer.

"The very thought of being alone with that fat control freak would give anybody the willies. What I'm trying to say is, we've just been presented with an opportunity to end this illegal occupation much sooner. Let's face it. The chances of some foreign military force coming in here to liberate us are slim to none."

Nicole glanced at her best friend puzzlingly.

"I can only imagine that Carragher has taken advantage of numerous women," Bridgette continued. "From what you've told me, this nutcase desires the love and affection of a 'real woman.' You can slip into that role without a hitch. Think about it Nicole. You've just become part of the resistance."

"I never thought of it that way," Nicole said as she drank her coffee. She was quite nervous. "I just don't want to do anything that will jeopardize Arielle."

"Simply play the part. And be discreet about it. Most likely, when Carragher begins to trust you, he'll lower his guard. He'll probably get you to work for him. Mailing correspondence, handling confidential files...jobs like that. Once you're in the inner sanctum, so to speak, keep your eyes and ears open. If at all possible, try to find out who the members of the resistance are in the city here.

*****

The booming, ear-piercing roar of the engines of three massive Lockheed Hercules planes had a range of a couple of kilometers. Frank Carragher, Major Toombs, Lt.-Colonel Mullen as well as a handful of high-ranking NAP and British Army officers stood by as the huge wheels of the Norwegian Air Force planes landed on the tarmac at the Kamloops Airport.

A group of six members of the British Parachute Regiment stood rigidly at attention. Brian Vance was among them. It was difficult to stay focused in the burning August sun. Colonel Bjorn Karlsen walked down the steps of one of the Hercules planes. A dozen Norwegian Army officers were with him. One by one, Norwegian troops unloaded off of the three planes. Vance studied their fair Nordic features; blonde and light brown hair, blue eyes. Like him, many were young men who enlisted simply out of a sense of nationalism or perhaps a desire to see the world. Most wanted nothing to do with the conflict that was ravaging every corner of the globe. They just did what they had to in order to survive.

Karlsen and his officers walked up to Carragher, Toombs and Mullen.

"Good afternoon Colonel Karlsen." Carragher greeted the Norwegians with a polite, professional smile. "Welcome to Kamloops. I trust your journey here was good."

"It's a short trip from Edmonton to here," Karlsen said.

"Colonel, I'm not sure if you've ever met Lieutenant Colonel Allister Mullen. He's the commanding officer of the local contingent of the UN force here. British Parachute Regiment."

"I don't believe that I have," Karlsen said as he shook Mullen's hand. "I have trained with some Paras before. I certainly have a high degree of respect for your outfit."

"Well, you know the Paras are undoubtedly one of the toughest elite units on the planet," Mullen responded a bit vainly.

"Colonel Karlsen, this here is Major Dan Toombs. "Major Toombs is in charge of the North American Police contingent for the Thompson-Nicola District."

Toombs and Karlsen shook hands.

"It's a wonderful feeling knowing that we will be working with some very professional, highly knowledgeable people," Karlsen stated as he looked around at the other Norwegian officers, who nodded in agreement.

"I just spoke with General Nilsson," Carragher stated. "If this country ever hopes to live long and prosper, as they say in North America, it is imperative to root out and eradicate all troublemakers and terrorists. Your troops will be lodged on base here along with the British and NAP forces. We have a beautiful old house close to downtown reserved for you and your officers. Please, come with us and we will help you get settled in."

Chapter 46

Nicole sat wearily in the backseat of a car driven by two NAP intelligence officers. From where she sat, it was obvious that her hometown had changed dramatically since the time she'd last walked through it as a free woman. Many of the storefronts that had added a sense of charming character to the downtown core were boarded-up and abandoned. There were checkpoints everywhere. It was a bright, sunny late summer's day. The agents drove up to Frank Carragher's home in Westsyde. The man and woman, their faces devoid of emotion, exited the car. The female agent opened the back door. Nicole got out of the car and took in her surroundings. It felt strange being back in civilization after a long hiatus. Carragher walked out onto the doorstep.

"Good evening," Carragher said warmly. "You may go back now. I have it from here."

"Sir, are you sure..." the male agent asked.

"It's quite alright sergeant." Carragher was impressed by the exquisite blouse and skirt that Nicole was wearing. "Please come inside, Nicole."

A bit edgy, Nicole followed her host into the spacious, mansion-like home. It was gorgeous. He certainly had expensive tastes. A huge staircase went up to the second floor. Beautiful paintings that cost more than many working-class folks made in a year hung from the walls.

Carragher sensed her nervousness.

"Nicole, you don't have to be afraid of me. Despite what many people say, I'm quite a friendly, approachable individual. As I said earlier, do as you're told and there will be no problems."

"Have you ever been married?" Nicole asked Carragher. She was trying to put on a good front.

"Once...a long time ago."

"So was I. Hadn't dated anybody until I met..." she missed Jake so much it pained her to even think of him. "Never mind. It's all in the past. So, what are we doing this evening?"

"Dinner is being served in roughly an hour's time. In the interim, we don't we go sit in the living room?"

Nicole followed Carragher into the home's large living room. Carragher walked over to the bar, which was stocked with at least thirty different types of liquors and spirits.

"Would you care for a drink?" Carragher asked.

"I most certainly would. Vodka and orange?"

"Coming right up."

Carragher took down a quart of Smirnoff. He opened up the small refrigerator located underneath the bar and removed a container of orange juice. The district administrator then poured half vodka and half orange juice into a glass and stirred well. Next, he fixed a Scotch on the rocks for himself. Drinks in hand, Carragher sat down beside Nicole on a plush living room couch.

Nicole took her drink and carefully sipped. Every drop of the sharp-tasting alcoholic drink made her feel good. Although not generally a drinker, Nicole did occasionally like to imbibe.

"This is great, Mr. Carragher."

"Happy that you like it. Nicole, I just want to establish one important thing before we go any further. Please call me Frank. Only my subordinates address me as Mr. Carragher. You're neither one of them nor are you some skanky little tramp who's only good for one thing."

"So what exactly am I to you, Frank?"

Carragher studied the younger woman's vivacious thighs and bare legs, becoming very aroused in the process.

"A very attractive, intelligent woman whom I can receive pleasure from and return pleasure to. Also, somebody with the brainpower to assist me in running this vast region. According to the reports I've read, you're reformed and renounced all of your old ways."

"I felt that it was time to possible choose a different path." Nicole had an uncanny ability to play others like fools. "I just want to know what I can do to help the government."

"Don't worry about that now. I will ensure that your skills are used in the right area." Carragher stroked Nicole's leg and put his fingers through her hair. His advances made her feel nauseas, but it was all part of the game.

"Frank, when I am going to be allowed to see my daughter?"

"Patience," he replied in a relaxed tone. It will happen soon enough."

*****

The group of rebels had been laying low since the last attack in Barriere. With the skies constantly abuzz with aircraft and UAVs, venturing out into the bush to collect and hunt food was particularly risky. Under a bright, starry sky, Mallory and Sarah Jane sat near the entrance to the abandoned mine. The daily apprehension and volatility of life in the mountains had begun to take its toll on each of them. Although Mallory felt that she was fighting for the right reasons, the young law student continued to worry somewhat about the two NAP troopers she had killed at the checkpoint as well as on the bridge. Sarah Jane was slowly becoming comfortable with the handling of firearms. The two close friends sat and talked in the refreshing night air.

"Come to think of it, this is the first time you and I have gotten together to talk in ages," Sarah Jane stated. "It's so quiet out here. Peaceful."

"I just hope we can survive the incoming winter," Mallory said. "It's truly hard to believe how much this conflict has changed all of us. I'm definitely a different person now than I was a year ago. I'm more strong-willed. I hate to admit it, but I've become more callous as well."

"It's the only way to survive through this. Do you remember how we met?"

"How could I forget that day?" Mallory replied with an embarrassed smile. "I still can't believe I actually got lost trying to find the classroom for Introduction to Canadian Law. If it hadn't have been for you, I would have spent all day wandering around."

Sarah Jane lay back beside Mallory on the ground, which was cushioned by a heavy blanket of pine needles.

"There isn't a day goes by when I don't think about the way things were and how they will never be that way again," Sarah Jane said sadly. "It crushes me to say this, but I won't be shocked if my family didn't survive this fiery ordeal. I just hope I get to find out sooner rather than later. Although I'd love to get back to Vancouver, I don't realistically expect it to happen anytime soon."

"I wonder what every one of us is going to do once this conflict is over. I personally cannot wait to see every one of those traitorous politicians, bankers and bureaucrats who plotted to destroy Canada and the United States swinging from lampposts."

"It's impossible to say exactly what will happen," Sarah Jane stated. "I know one thing though; we simply aren't, at least not right away, going to be able to resume our studies, enter law careers and make millions of dollars."

"Sad but true. I'm just trying to take each day at a time Sarah Jane. It gets too hard on the head worrying about the future. I've just been thankful to God for getting me through all of this."

"I can't blindly believe that an all-powerful supreme being controls this planet as well as the destinies of seven billion human beings. You'd have to provide me with substantial evidence that God exists. But I understand where you're coming from. There's probably a higher power out there in the galaxy somewhere."

Chapter 47

Bob Hunt and his fellow patriots knew that it would only be a matter of time before the district government retaliated against the city's population. The five men had been bracing themselves for this inevitable backlash. A total lockdown had been imposed upon Kamloops at eleven o'clock the previous night. All residents were under strict orders to remain in their homes until further notice. Over a dozen NAP and UN helicopters buzzed loudly in the sky over the sprawling central British Columbia city. Each one of Kamloops' twenty-seven incorporated neighborhoods was sealed off.

Robert Hunt peered through the large window of his living room. An ATF Dingo 2 drove slowly down his street. An observant gunner whose hands gripped a .50 caliber machine gun sat in the turret. Soldiers were going door-to-door checking residences. All of a sudden, Hunt heard a rapt knock at his door. Barbara trembled in fear.

"Oh my God, Bob. What are they going to do?"

"Absolutely nothing," Hunt replied as if he wasn't all that concerned. "Let them take a look around. There's nothing here that would interest them."

Hunt opened the front door. Two UN soldiers dressed in heavy battle gear and grasping Heckler & Koch HK416 rifles stood on his doorstep. On their shoulders was the patch of the International Security Assistance Force as well as a small version of the Norwegian flag. Their nametags said Eriksen and Friedberg.

"Good day, Sir." Eriksen spoke politely in a thick Scandinavian accent. "By the authority of the North American government, we are ordered to check every home in this city for weapons."

Hunt had prepared himself for this exact scenario.

"Come inside."

The young soldiers looked around. Barbara glared upon the intruders revoltingly. It was as if they were expecting her horrified reaction and merely wanted to do their job and get out quickly. The Norwegians conducted a quick check of the main closets and rooms of the house. To the relief of the Hunts, they did not go any further. Hunt couldn't help but feel somewhat guilty for having to put his fellow city residents through all of this. But these were desperate times and in order to achieve victory, this had to happen.

*****

Lately, those disturbing dreams that had been haunting Jake for months in his sleep decided to return. The memory of hearing Nicole's traumatized voice-the last contact he'd had with her-tore away at him. Jake pulled the sleeping bag up around him. It was approaching September and although the days were still very hot, nights could get quite chilly. The rebels were doing more hunting these days. They also conducted reconnaissance missions on roads in the vicinity of their hideout.

Soon, they planned to ambush one of the NAP armored personnel carriers that frequently patrolled the roads. The more pressing issue at hand was the prospect of having to tough out a cold, snowy winter in the mountains.

It would be an insurmountable task for sure. In his head, Jake constantly devised schemes about how he would sneak back into Kamloops and rescue Nicole and Arielle-that is if they hadn't been moved or, Heaven forbid, killed. Jake stared up at the ceiling of the dark, abandoned mine.

"God, you've probably figured out by now that I'm not a particularly religious man, but if you can hear me, my only request is that you watch over Nicole and Arielle and keep them safe."

Chapter 48

The lockdown remained in effect well into the next day. Only those residents with special permits were allowed to leave their homes. The intensive search of every occupied dwelling in Kamloops turned up over one hundred firearms-many of them family heirlooms owned by elderly people-as well as canisters of gunpowder, ammunition and other explosive materials. Robert Hunt sat quietly, his hands wrapped around a steaming cup of coffee. It had been days since he had spoken with Jeff and Ben Hinton, Marty Smith, Chris Templeton or Father Tuck. Hunt feared that one or more of them could have been swept up in the searches. Facing the prospect of torture, anybody-even the most mentally tough-would likely spill the beans. Should that happen, there would be no hope for an organized resistance movement now or in the future.

"Bob, come here now." There was alarm and urgency in Barbara's voice.

Hunt got up from the table and went into the living room. On TV, Frank Carragher's all-pervading eyes and sagging jowls dominated the screen eerily reminiscent of Big Brother in George Orwell's 1984.

"Greetings, dear members of the proletariat. Since taking my post as administrator of your vast, very beautiful region, I have been a fair, objective and most importantly, a lenient ruler. I have permitted all of you a reasonable amount of freedom of movement, the right to assemble and even bring forth complaints and petitions to my office."

The Hunts could tell that there was something genuinely sinister about the man just by looking at him.

"And this is how you repay my leniency, my generosity," Carragher continued. "There are some of you hidden amongst a population of roughly 123,000 souls who have no respect for the law. You will stop at nothing to undermine the federal government's presence here. You senselessly murder four North American Police officers and a captain in the federal department of corrections. Then you believe you can hide weapons from my troops. I cannot pinpoint exactly who is responsible, but due to your selfish and reckless actions, fifteen of your fellow citizens are about to die."

The screen switched to the football field located on the southern edge of Kamloops. Major Toombs and Lt.-Colonel Mullen, along with a group of NAP and British Paras, stood about twenty feet away from fifteen city residents that were lined up about a foot apart. For the Hunts, it was almost surreal having to watch innocent civilians ranging from teenagers to old men, their faces terrified, about to die. A mother and her teenage daughter held each other as they cried profusely.

The fortyish man in the centre of the lineup was Gerald McCann. The woman and teenage girl to the left were McCann's wife Laura and daughter Ilia. Hunt's adrenaline shot up. His mouth was dry. Clear thoughts were quickly muddied. Among the condemned was Charles O'Brien. O'Brien had served for thirty-five years in the Canadian Army on a variety of peacekeeping missions. O'Brien, who was pushing eighty, was also an avid gun collector.

Brian Vance felt sick to his stomach as he gripped his assault rifle. The palms of his hands were oozing sweat. The novice paratrooper had been selected to be part of the firing squad. He stood alongside six of his fellow paras. There was no way in Hell he could bring himself to do this.

"On my command!" Mullen yelled.

The firing squad raised their rifles. Though it could very well result in a court martial or, at the very least, a severe tongue-lashing by his superiors-Vance decided to discreetly shoot at the ground behind the victims.

Hunt's body contorted with rage. His blood pressure shot up like a rocket. Hopefully he wouldn't have a heart attack. Her face as white as a sheet, Barbara slunk into the couch. Hunt was scared that his wife of four decades would faint. It killed both of them to watch Ilia fall to her knees begging for her life.

"Please...please...don't kill us!" The young girl pleaded. Laura knelt down beside her daughter.

"Fire at will!" Mullen commanded in his booming voice.

The Paras unleashed a firestorm of bullets that ripped mercilessly through the bodies of the fifteen city residents. Vance shot around them. Barbara became weaker. She felt lightheaded as she got up off of the couch.

"Bob, I'm going to be sick."

Barbara ran into the bathroom and shut the door behind her. Hunt shut off the television. He sat there, the life completely drained out of him. As soon as the lockdown was lifted, he would be meeting with the other members of the resistance cell. Hunt had just witnessed the government of North America, with the assistance of the United Nations, commit a senseless act of genocide. He hoped and prayed that the silver lining to come out of this horrific event would be a total insurrection by the city's residents.

Chapter 49

Father Tuck felt as though he had been bearing the brunt of the turmoil taking place all throughout the Thompson-Nicola District. Each day, the office at Sacred Heart as well as his own cell phone, was inundated with calls from parishioners as well as members of the city's other Christian denominations. Tuck frequently received requests to pray for those imprisoned, sick and missing. In addition, he was always counselling people.

The veteran priest had always believed he would be called to a life of serving others. Although it was a life he enjoyed immensely, it was starting to burn him out. Tuck was aware that Nicole Clare had been sent to reside at the home of Frank Carragher. He knew exactly what the power-mad administrator's true intentions were. Tuck was hanging on to the hope that Nicole would convince Carragher that she was genuinely in love with him. Gaining Carragher's complete trust would be a vital step in bringing his little fiefdom crashing to the ground.

Tuck had spent the past few days visiting and sometimes praying with the detainees. As of yet, he had not been permitted to meet with any of the children. Tuck was in the midst of cleaning chalices when Robert Hunt and Marty Smith walked into the church.

"Good afternoon gentlemen," Tuck said.

"Father, is there someplace quiet we can talk?" Smith asked.

"Yes there is. Follow me."

Hunt and Smith followed Tuck through the church vestry, down a flight of steps into the basement.

They proceeded down a small corridor, at the end of which was a heavy wooden door. Tuck fished some keys out of his pocket and opened it. The room, located at the back of the church, was being used for storage. Even if federal agents had placed bugs inside of the church, this one particular place was tucked away and therefore easy to overlook. The three men sat down on some old chairs.

"I assume you've figured out by now that we successfully carried out our first mission," Smith stated.

Tuck was still reeling from the horrible images he and thousands of others had been forced to watch on television.

"This is a very complicated matter," Tuck said solemnly. "While the Lord does condone the use of violence, we cannot allow any more innocent blood to be shed. It was inevitable that this would happen. Charles O'Brien grew up in this church. Bill and Maria Sherran have been members of Sacred Heart since moving to Kamloops in 1987. Satan is alive and well in this world and it is our duty to stop him."

"I echo your sentiments," Hunt said. "We are slowly trying to bring more people into the fold. Is there any new intel to report from the jail?"

"They've found a replacement for Ron Storey."

"That quickly?! Who is it?" Hunt asked curiously.

"Janet Paynter."

"Oh Christ!" Smith grumbled. He quickly remembered where he was. "Sorry Father."

"You are forgiven my son," Tuck said to him.

"She's every bit as heartless," Hunt said. "My source inside the prison has told me she's very hard on her own guards."

"That wouldn't surprise me," Tuck replied. "Are you aware that she pitches for the other team as well?"

"That's obvious," Smith said.

*****

Brian Vance did not expect his 'discreet' show of defiance to go unnoticed by the all-pervading eyes of his superiors. The young paratrooper stood ramrod straight, his muscled frame trembling under the penetrating glare of Captain Sean Wynne. Vance had been summoned into the administration offices of the British Army, which were located within the Kamloops Airport. Sergeant-Major Kempling looked on as Wynne went up one side of Vance and down the other.

"Private Vance, do you have any fucking idea how much money Her Majesty's government spends on training each and every member of one of our nation's most storied and renowned regiments?" Wynne kept his eyes inches from Vance's face. "What the hell possessed you to fuck up so badly out there?"

If Vance explained to his superior officer the true reason for his actions, he would be in a world of pain and suffering. In all likelihood, he'd be charged with high treason and sedition and could quite possibly find himself in front of a firing squad.

"I don't know, Sir...I just tensed up. I'm sorry."

"You never say you're sorry! That's the biggest sign of weakness and I will not tolerate any weakness or cowardice amongst my troops. Perhaps you're becoming softer. Feeling sympathy for the fine, upstanding citizens of this city?" Wynne said sarcastically.

Vance stared straight ahead.

"Because if that's the case, I will personally make sure that you get buried so deep you will never see the light of day again."

At that moment, Mullen entered the office. Wynne turned to him.

"Sir," he said as he addressed the base commander.

"Private Vance, is this true? Did you, shall we say, freeze up?" Mullen asked him.

"Yes, Sir. I can't explain what happened."

Mullen studied his face. It was a sincere one.

"Hmm...this would not be the first time such an incident has happened during the long history of the British Army."

"You made a poor judgment call the other day. Unfortunately, in this line of work, such a severe lack of judgment can cost the lives of others. Private Vance, for the next week, I am confining you to barracks. You will clean, wash clothes, I might even get you to work in our offices a bit. In seven days' time,

hopefully you will have learned your lesson as you will be returned to active duty. Dismissed."
Vance saluted the two officers before leaving the office.

Chapter 50

Mallory's skinny frame shivered in the predawn chill. In her hands she grasped a 'liberated' British rifle. The band of rebels had been hunkered down since the wee hours of the morning. They entrenched themselves into positions amongst the sparsely-forested hillside that flanked a lesser-used paved road that wound through the mountains. Beyond the hillsides were vast spruce forests and rugged mountain peaks that jutted high into the sky.

While their comrades acted as sentries, Kevin and Jake had planted an improvised explosive device inside of a hard plastic culvert located at the intersection of where the road met three other roads. To construct the improvised explosive device (IED), Kevin installed wires into a smartphone, which were then inserted into a brick of C4. Jake and Kevin placed the C4 on top of a tightly-packed barrel full of a volatile mixture of diesel fuel and fertilizer. Once the IED had been packed inside, they sealed both ends of the culvert.

Calvin crouched down amongst the undergrowth as best as he could. Neil was beside him. The best friends and fellow freedom fighters positioned the light machinegun that had been taken from the British supply truck. Jake was situated twenty meters away. He grasped a LAW Rocket. Sarah Jane stayed close to Mallory. The generally peaceful environmentalist and social activist was beginning to realize that she may have no option but to fight. A lone

NAP armored personnel carrier drove into view. It was headed east. Kevin grasped a cellular phone in his hand.

The head of the driver was barely visible. The gunner was very well protected by an imposing turret.

Kevin steadied himself. The APC appeared as one of the thousands of 'surplus' military vehicles that had been donated to law enforcement agencies across Canada and the United States in the years preceding the North American Union. It looked like a former Canadian Forces Cougar. The APC slowed down as it drove toward the four-way stop. Kevin kept his fingers inches away from the cell phone's keypad.

As the APC got within three meters of the stop sign, Kevin dialled a number. Four seconds later, the ground underneath of the right side of the road erupted following an ear-splitting explosion. The robust, heavily armored vehicle was lifted a good ten feet into the air before being promptly tossed violently onto its head into an adjacent ditch. Jake's ears strained to hear what sounded faintly like helicopters. Fearful adrenaline overcame his body. All of a sudden, two Apache attack helicopters appeared over the mountains.

"Retreat!" Jake yelled.

As the insurgents scattered to the safety of the heavily forested mountains, the Apaches unleashed a torrent of gunfire into the hillside. Neil was cut down instantly.

"Neil!" Calvin yelled as he went to assist his fallen comrade. Kevin grabbed his nephew.

"Calvin, he's dead! Come on."

Sarah Jane quickly found her fine motor skills going instantly out of whack. She dropped the AR-15 and fled up the hill, her heart pounding wildly. Suddenly, bullets slammed into the dusty earth all around her.

Paralyzed with fear, the young woman couldn't move. Calvin sprinted further up the hillside and took cover amongst a cluster of ponderosa pines. He grasped the light machinegun. Before the feisty youth could even aim the machinegun, a Hellfire missile swooshed out of the rocket pods of one of the Apaches. It struck the ground barely a foot away from Calvin, blasting his body to bits.

Kevin quickly scooped up the light machinegun. As if it was nothing to him, the bear of a man aimed and fired a succession of 7.62 rounds into the helicopter's cockpit. The heavily-armed chopper swerved crazily in the air for a minute before crashing into the hillside and exploding into a ball of flame.

The pilot of the second gunship hovered in the air as he observed a panicky Mallory moving as fast as her legs would take her. The gunner sat in the front.

"Roger One Niner...got one of them in my sights now," the pilot said into the headset on his helmet.

Mallory was out of breath by the time she reached the crest of the hill.

"Oh my God, Sarah Jane!" Mallory watched her best friend clinging to the ground further down the hill. Although she desperately wanted to help her, there was nothing she could do.

The M230 chain gun of the second Apache focused on Mallory.

"I got you now you little bitch!" the pilot said through gritted teeth.

Without warning, Jake appeared from behind a cluster of trees. He raised the LAW rocket. The pilot and gunner looked on in terror as a missile was thrust directly at them. In no time at all, the powerful air beast was reduced to a shower of sparks and thousands of tiny pieces of burning metal that cascaded to the ground below.

Kevin, Jake and Mallory took advantage of the small window of opportunity to retreat further into the mountains. Two NAP Bell 412 helicopters flew over the mountains and landed on the road. Eight NAP troopers got out of each of them, including Major Toombs. While half of the troopers struggled to get the back hatch of the upside-down APC opened, the others searched the hillside. Two of the troopers, their faces obscured by masks, came upon Sarah Jane. It took a lot of effort, but the troopers were finally able to get the hatch open. Eight shaken, bruised but otherwise unscathed colleagues quickly made their way out of the wrecked vehicle.

The troopers brought a struggling Sarah Jane over to Major Toombs.

"Sir, this is the only one we were able to capture," a corporal stated. "The remaining enemy combatants are either dead or have fled into the mountains."

"I can see that, corporal," Toombs snapped back. Toombs looked upon Sarah Jane, who glared at him with eyes of contempt.

"What is your name?"

"Go to Hell!"

"Take her directly to the detention centre," Toombs ordered. He surveyed the vast, awe-inspiring wilderness laid out in front of him like a painting. "And as for Jake Scribner, his days are numbered."

Chapter 51

There was a slight chill in the temperature of the room. It caused an already stressed, frightened Sarah Jane to shiver. Everything had happened so fast she could not fully grasp the impact of the situation. A torrent of emotions rushed through her mind. *Were they going to kill her? Would they hunt down the remnants of the group?* Since arriving at the re-education centre, Sarah Jane had been locked up inside of a small room. She was interrogated and verbally abused by her captors. The environmentalist breathed deeply, sweated as Janet Paynter hovered over her. Toombs and a broad-shouldered NAP three-striper named Gardiner stood on opposite sides of her. Officer Stanford stood guard by the door.

"Sarah Jane Pearce. Born and raised in Vancouver. Went to the University of British Columbia. Moved to Kamloops last year to attend law school. Parents are Michael and Rachel Pearce. You have one sister, Hannah." It was as if Paynter knew Sarah Jane's entire life story. "Active in the environmental movement. Arrested two years ago during a rally against a pipeline project near Prince George. We know everything about you rebel scum. There is nothing that you can hide from us. Now, are you going to tell us exactly what we want to know? Regardless of your defiance, we will extract the information out of you. We can either do this the easy way or the hard way."

Sarah Jane felt the pressure closing in all around her. It appeared as though she might be tortured. She made a pledge to herself not to say anything that would give her friends away.

"There's a little rule around here. Nobody fucks with Captain Paynter. When I instruct a detainee to do something, they better damn well comply or else there will be serious consequences."

"I'd be interested in learning how a prissy city gal such as yourself ended up in the company of Jake Scribner," Toombs said. Like Paynter, he was also receiving the silent treatment from Sarah Jane. Infuriated, Toombs locked eyes with the young woman. "You'd better start answering questions or else it's going to get really nasty in here. Tell us where you acquired those weapons."

Sarah Jane refused to answer.

"So you want to play that game," Paynter said in her gruff, almost manly voice. "We'll be more than happy to accommodate you. Sergeant Gardiner, do what you do best."

A man of few words, Gardiner, ripped to shreds with an intimidating shaved head and glaring eyes, roughly picked Sarah Jane up from her chair and dragged her down a corridor into a janitorial room. Paynter and Toombs followed. Stanford watched, a slight look of displeasure in his eyes. Gardiner forced a struggling Sarah Jane's face inches from a sink filled with water.

"Tell us where you acquired your weapons!" Gardiner screamed.

"No."

Gardiner submerged Sarah Jane's head into the water. Overwhelmed by a drowning sensation, she struggled to breathe, thrashing violently. After about half a minute, Gardiner removed Sarah Jane's head from the water. She gasped frenziedly for air.

"Are you ready to talk to us now?"

Sarah Jane remained tight-lipped.

"You leave me little choice," Gardiner said before dunking her head back into the sink.

Toombs and Paynter observed as Sarah Jane thrashed. Water flew everywhere.

"Major, what do we do in the event that she outright refuses to talk?" Paynter asked.

"This one isn't all that tough," Toombs replied. "She'll give the game away."

Gardiner pulled Sarah Jane's head from the sink.

"If you insist on your insolence, I will have no choice but to…"

"Wait!" Sarah Jane shouted.

"You wish to talk?" Paynter asked.

Sarah Jane nodded.

"Stanford!" Paynter barked. "Get her a towel."

"Yes ma'am," Stanford replied as he opened up a cabinet and took out a large towel. He handed it to Sarah Jane, who dried off her soaked face and hair as best she could.

"Alright," Toombs said. "Where did you acquire those weapons to commit atrocities against the federal government?"

Sarah Jane felt as though she was committing a major breach of trust by divulging the truth about the ambush months ago that resulted in the deaths of two British soldiers. She feared that by telling them the truth, it could lead to her being executed.

"Back, I think it was in May, we were somewhere out in the woods practicing maneuvers. A supply truck stopped on the highway. Two British soldiers got out and walked into the woods."

Toombs listened. He knew exactly what she was talking about.

"I had never experienced anything like this before in my life," Sarah Jane continued. "All I can say is it was a kill or be killed situation."

"If I recall, there were several items of weaponry stolen from that vehicle," Toombs stated. "Assault rifles, a machinegun, LAW rockets, lots of ammunition…but you had more gear, including C4. Now, you better tell us who supplied you with plastic explosives or else the pain and suffering that you'll be forced to endure will be ten times worse than anything you've experienced so far."

Sarah Jane swallowed hard. She was in the midst of a tricky situation.

"Honestly, I will tell you everything that I know. I've never met this individual, but somebody named Shamus gave Jake, Neil and Calvin some supplies. His last name is either O'Reilly or O'Reagan. I've been told he's an old Irish Republican Army fighter."

"Where does he live?" Paynter asked.

"To the best of my knowledge, somewhere off of Highway 97." Sarah hoped and prayed that her answers would be sufficient enough.

"I know your group has some kind of hidden lair up in the mountains," Toombs said. "Tell us exactly where it is."

"To be honest, there isn't just one. There are several. I don't know this area very well so I can't tell you exact locations."

"You're still playing games Ms. Pierce. Perhaps some time locked up will help you to remember." Toombs turned to Paynter. "Captain, she's all yours from here."

"Major, this traitorous little piece of shit deserves nothing more than to be placed in front of a firing squad. She's only liable to cause trouble in here," Paynter stated.

"Off the record, I couldn't agree more with you," Toombs said. "But as you're well aware, we are required to follow policy and procedure. Keeping her alive will be much more beneficial to us in the long run."

Chapter 52

Jake, Mallory and Kevin sat quietly inside of the old abandoned mine. A solitary candle broke diminutively through the thick darkness. After destroying the second Apache gunship, the three remaining rebels fled deep into the unending mountain forest. Mallory firmly believed that God had protected them from the legions of pursuing aircraft that occupied the skies overhead. It was deathly quiet inside of the group's living quarters. The stale granola bars the three downtrodden and depressed rebels chewed on were barely edible. Kevin held his head in anguish. Calvin had been the only relative he knew that was still alive.

"I told my brother that I'd watch out for him. Keep him safe from harm." Kevin was at the point of breaking down in tears. "Guess I failed miserably there."

Mallory patted Kevin's shoulder.

"Kevin, don't be so hard on yourself. There is no way any of us could have anticipated the outcome of that attack." Mallory could not shake the images of Sarah Jane lying on the ground. She was unsure as to whether her best friend was dead or had been captured by government forces. "I shudder to think what happened to Sarah Jane. If she was taken alive, I can only imagine the things that will be done to her."

"It's tough to say," Jake stated. "She definitely will be interrogated. Those bastards will want to know the exact location of our base. Even though Sarah Jane is a very intelligent young lady, she doesn't function particularly well under pressure. Rest assured, they will resort to any means, including torture, to extract the information they want. You have to remember. There is no rule of law anymore. No Geneva Convention, no constitution in either Canada or the United States to prevent such abuses from happening."

"I'm concerned about that as well, Jake," Kevin said. "It isn't that I believe Sarah Jane will intentionally sell us out. But she's likely to crack under duress."

*****

The drab blue jumpsuit was too big for her small frame. She reeked of the delousing powder a group of heckling guards had poured all over her wet, naked body. Sarah Jane quivered with fright and uneasiness as two guards escorted her into H Block. Stanford was posted inside of the pod that controlled access to the unit was well as each individual cell. A cell door opened following a buzzing sound.

"Bridgette, your new cellmate has arrived," One of the officers stated.

Sarah Jane was ushered inside. The cell was small. A bit cramped. A pretty, plain-faced woman in her early thirties sat on the top bunk reading the Bible. Sarah Jane felt as though she was a visitor from another planet. Bridgette got down off of the bunk. The cell door was slammed shut.

"Hi, my name is Bridgette. And you are—

"Sarah Jane."

"When were you arrested? Are you from around here?"

Sarah Jane sat down on the bottom bunk.

"I'm from Vancouver. I just moved here to go to law school," she explained. "My friend and I have been living in the mountains since the end of April. We were part of a group."

"My previous cellmate was taken out of here about a week ago. Her name was Nicole."

"Nicole who?"

"Clare. You probably wouldn't—

Sarah Jane's eyes went wide with excitement.

"I have never met Nicole personally but I know her fiancé."

"Jake Scribner?" Bridgette was shocked.

Sarah Jane nodded.

"You're part of the resistance!" A smile lit up Bridgette's face.

"That's correct. Do you know where Nicole is now?"

"She works for the district administrator's office," Bridgette explained. "In case you didn't already know, his name is Frank

Carragher. He likes to use some of the female inmates for sexual pleasure."

"Doesn't surprise me."

"Sarah Jane, I'm going to tell you something. It's terrifying, but you must be informed." Bridgette sighed. "That head guard, the butch-looking officer there."

"You're referring to Paynter. She's nuts."

"She certainly is. Anyway, Paynter and about a dozen other guards operate a sex trafficking ring inside of the facility. They sell women to everybody from high federal government Officials right down to those NAP thugs. Make a small fortune from it too. I realize that you're traumatized, but I just want you to know what's been happening in this place."

"Thanks for the heads up. I guess I will have to stand my guard against her."

"Sarah Jane, where is Jake Scribner right now?"

"Hopefully not dead. Early this morning, we ambushed an armored patrol using a culvert bomb. Little did we know that there were two Apache helicopters waiting to spring a counter-ambush upon us," Sarah Jane elucidated. "My two friends Calvin and Neil were cut down in a hail of bullets. Jake and Kevin as well as my best friend Mallory, whom I met in law school, fled into the mountains. That's the last thing I remember. It's all a blur after that."

Chapter 53

The day had finally arrived; Nicole was going to be reunited with Arielle. The single mother and freedom activist sat nervously in the foyer of Frank Carragher's enormous home. Over the past couple of weeks, Nicole had been kept busy filing paperwork as well as writing press releases that were pure propaganda. Although Carragher had not been overly aggressive in his advances-at least not yet-Nicole felt quite uncomfortable being alone with him.

It would only be a matter of time before he expected-make that demanded-her to tend to his needs, so to speak. Nicole, going through the motions to ensure her own survival and, most importantly, that of her daughter's, continued to cling to the faint hope that somehow, somewhere, her knight in shining armor would arrive back in town, eliminate all of the villains and sweep her up in his arms. Most real-life stories did not have such a glamorous fairy tale ending.

Nicole sat still as she heard the sound of a vehicle pulling up in front of the house. She tried to keep her emotions in check. Outside, two officials from the federal corrections department opened the backseat of an unmarked car they were driving. Arielle, a bit bewildered, stepped out of the back of the car. Carragher was standing on the doorstep.

"Take her inside," the district administrator ordered.

The federal agents escorted Arielle into the foyer. Nicole's knees buckled. Her little girl-her one and only child-appeared much more grown up since the last time she'd seen her.

That wasn't the only thing different about Arielle. Gone was the happy-go-lucky sparkle in the child's eyes as well as her million-dollar smile. Arielle appeared distant, as if she'd been brainwashed.

The correctional officials turned and left. Overwhelmed by a combination of exuberance and tearful joy, Nicole embraced Arielle in her arms. Immediately she noticed that the bond they'd once had wasn't there.

"So here you are." Nicole smiled through the river of tears that ran down her face. "You have no idea how much I missed you. At least you're being well fed in there. What do you and the other children do all day?"

"We attend citizenship classes. The instructors teach us about the Fatherland and how President Asher loves and cares for each and every citizen of his great republic. They once told me that you were a dangerous enemy of the state who deserved no mercy."

Oh, had she ever been brainwashed. Nicole had been given back a completely different little girl. She only hoped that it wouldn't be too late to save her.

"Don't worry honey. I have changed a lot. And because of that, we are going to be a family again. Let's sit down, shall we?"

Nicole pointed to the large chesterfield. Mother and daughter sat down.

"Arielle, do you know Mr. Carragher?"

"Our illustrious administrator," Arielle said respectfully. "We have learned so much about you in our classes."

"It warms my heart to hear that," the pompous, domineering bureaucrat said. "Your mother has been serving me well. In the not-too-distant future, you too will be chosen to serve your country."

"But you don't have to worry about that now," Nicole said with a smile as she put her arms around Arielle. She could sense that Arielle was not comfortable with it.

"I have a little present for you."

Nicole reached inside of a fancy shopping bag and retrieved a gorgeous porcelain doll.

"I know how much you love dolls. At least you used to."

Arielle looked over the doll, which had alluring eyes and auburn hair. It was encased inside of a plastic and cardboard package.

"Do they give you toys to play with?"

"No," Arielle answered.

"We are going to be living here with Mr. Carragher. It's amazing that you and I are together once more. That must make you happy."

"Just as long as you've changed your ways."

"Believe me dear, I have," Nicole bluffed. "And I did it for you."

Chapter 54

Shamus O'Reilly had been laying low since the start of the occupation of the Thompson-Nicola district. He'd not heard from any of the members of the resistance cell. O'Reilly wondered how they were fairing out or even if they had survived the past few months. Out of the blue, O'Reilly heard what sounded like helicopters approaching his ranch. The former IRA member had become quite paranoid living by himself out in the wilderness. He opened up a closet and took out an M16/UA2 rifle that had an attached grenade launcher.

O'Reilly rushed out onto the deck of his house just as two Apache attack helicopters flew toward the house. The choppers' nicknames were "Vulture" and "Death from Above." The Apaches belonged to the North American Police Air Division.

A pilot and gunner sat inside of the cockpit of Vulture. The pilot stared straight ahead as O'Reilly's house came into view.

"Vulture here. Coordinates fifty-four latitude, longitude seventy. Elevation, three-thousand, five-hundred and sixty-seven meters." The pilot spoke into the radio on his helmet. "Target is on the deck of the house armed."

"Engaged immediately," a voice came through the radio.

"Roger that. Going hot."

Vulture and Death from Above moved in closer. Vulture's gunner gripped the controls. He turned the helicopter's M230 chain gun with his helmet.

Suddenly, a grenade flew through the air. It missed Death from Above's right wing by a few inches before falling onto the ground and exploding.

"Take that you fascist pieces of shit!" O'Reilly yelled.

Both helicopters unleashed a torrent of thirty-millimeter bullets directly at O'Reilly. The aging IRA man was cut down in seconds. Next, the pilots fired Hellfire missiles into the house, blowing it to smithereens.

*****

Brian Vance had recently returned to his regular duties as a member of the British Parachute Regiment. For a week or so he'd been more or less an errand boy for Colonel Mullen. During that period, Vance had seen a side of the veteran army officer that troubled him deeply. Mullen, while acting very polite and professional, was in reality a closet sadist.

Vance had been largely shunned by most of his mates, although he and Pete Huggins remained close friends. It was a warm, early September day. Vance noticed the contrasting very cool and crisp nights that would precede what was promising to be a good old-fashioned Canadian winter. The two Paras managed to find a restaurant that still had its deck open.

As Vance and Huggins nursed cups of tea, Vance studied the faces of the local denizens that walked by. They wore expressions of fear, paranoia and silent rage against the foreign invaders that had taken over their lives and stripped them of their freedoms. As somebody who had always had a great amount of respect for Canadians, it struck a nerve inside of Vance. It sickened him to be seen not as a liberator but a murderer.

A young waitress walked over to the table carrying a tray with plates of fish and chips on it. She set the tray in front of the young paratroopers. The girl, no older than eighteen or nineteen, avoided eye contact with them as much as possible. Vance took a bite of the breaded fish.

"Tastes not too bad. Nothing like back home but good enough nonetheless."

Huggins started into his meal.

"Brian, what do you think got into you a couple of weeks back? You froze up."

"I prefer not to talk about it."

"It bothers you, doesn't it?"

"What bothers me?"

"Brian, don't get offended by what I'm about to say. You're an excellent soldier-there's no getting around that-but myself and the guys have noticed that you have a bit of a weak spot. Maybe you're just not cut out for the brutalities of war."

"Since when did you become an expert in the "brutalities of war?" Vance felt his blood pressure rising a notch. "It it's all the same to you, I don't exactly enjoy mowing down innocent civilians."

"They were not innocent. The NAP and Norwegian forces found weapons inside of all of their houses. They wouldn't hesitate to kill either one of us. If you want to get through this, you have to stop thinking that way. Besides, orders are orders."

"You don't think I already know that?" Vance nibbled on one of his French fries. If any of Vance's comrades knew exactly what was going through his mind, he'd be cited for treason and imprisoned. It was nearing the point where he couldn't hide his true feelings any longer.

Chapter 55

Becoming Frank Carragher's assistant/mistress had been a bit of a mixed blessing for Nicole. It enabled her to be reunited with Arielle. At the same time, she felt like a traitor to her family and country, even though she was merely faking in order to assist the growing resistance movement in the district. As a chilly rain fell outside, Nicole and Arielle huddled under a blanket sipping hot chocolate and watching the cartoons Arielle had once loved. Carragher had permitted Nicole to have the day off. Carragher wasn't in the mood to spend an entire day at the office and opted instead to go golfing with some high-ranking federal government officials who were visiting from Vancouver.

Carragher entered the house. He was wet and feeling miserable. Nicole went into the foyer to greet him.

"How were the links today?"

Carragher took off his jacket and hung it in a closet.

"First hour or two was amazing. Sun was shining. Looked like it was going to be a nice day. Then this godforsaken rain started. I hope you have dinner cooked because I'm starving."

"It's all in the oven. Meatloaf, baked potatoes and green beans fresh from the garden. Oh, and there's apple pie for dessert."

"One thing's for certain; you certainly know how to please a man…in more ways than one."

Carragher smiled lewdly. Nicole returned the gesture in kind. What pleased Nicole the most was the undeniable fact that her 'benefactor' was playing right into the trap she was slowly laying for him.

Carragher parked his hefty frame on a large armchair across from Nicole and Arielle.

"North American Police units have just obliterated the home of an individual who supplied weapons to your former boyfriend and his gang of domestic terrorists. Nothing left of the place except for a smoldering flame. I have teams out searching those mountains for every base and hideout they've been using. Even though you have completely renounced your old ways, I felt you should know about this."

Nicole stared blankly at the wall across from her. She fought viciously to choke back a sob. Betraying her emotions would be the death knell for both her and Arielle. Nicole was sickened at the thought of never being with the love of her life again."

"Jake was always like that. Believed he could beat the system. To be honest with you Frank, I can't believe I actually once loved that asshole."

Arielle was confused. She had fought against the brainwashing herself but was forced to succumb to it-at least partially.

'Is my mother serious or is she just making this up?'

Carragher got up off of his chair.

"Needless to say, I'm impressed with the progress you've made Nicole. Keep up the good work. Soon, you will be placed in a high position within the government. That will ensure stability for both you and your daughter."

■■■

Sarah Jane had not been having a particularly easy time adjusting to life locked up like a condemned criminal. Paynter and some of the female guards were consistently harassing and hitting on her. Sarah Jane worried constantly about Mallory but also Jake and Kevin, whom she had grown to love very much. For at least one hour each day, Sarah Jane was interrogated by NAP intelligence agents. They were not satisfied with the information she was giving them, most of which was false. Sarah Jane feared that the NAP would torture her into revealing the exact location of the abandoned mine where Jake, Kevin and Mallory were holed up in.

Sarah Jane picked away at the monotonous-looking food on her tray. It was noontime. She was exhausted from having to sit through three back-to-back 're-education classes'. Like Nicole before her, Sarah Jane had found a trusting friend in Bridgette Shaw. Sarah Jane felt for the devoted mother and wife.

"If I lose any more weight, I'm going to resemble a skeleton," Sarah Jane said.

"The food may not be glamorous, but you have to keep your strength up."

"Bridgette, do you believe that we will ever get out of here?"

"I wish I had the answer for that sweetie. Truly, I do. We just have to stay strong and keep praying every day."

Chapter 56

Brian Vance continued to find himself locked in an unrelenting battle of conscience. He could no longer abide being a party to the mistreatment, unlawful confinement and murder of innocent civilians. It troubled Vance even more to see his own comrades treating local women like whores. Dressed in a buttoned shirt and blue jeans, Vance strolled through downtown Kamloops. It was a very warm fall day, a whopping twenty-two degrees Celsius. With the recent attacks on North American Police troopers, Vance understood the potential risks of being outside of the wire, so to speak. The devout Roman Catholic prayed to Jesus and Mary to protect him through this period of great tribulation. Vance stopped in front of Sacred Heart Church. It was doubtful as to whether the parish priest would be around. All the same, he needed desperately to talk to someone.

Vance entered. He dipped his right index finger and middle fingers in the small dish of holy water just inside of the church and blessed himself. A tall, somewhat stocky priest walked down the aisle and greeted Vance.

"Good day, Father."

Upon hearing the young man's Cockney accent, Tuck knew immediately that he was from out of town, quite possibly a member of the Royal British Parachute Regiment.

"How are you doing son?" Tuck kept his distance. If this kid was indeed an intelligence agent, he would be sure to trip him up.

"Father, I…"

"It's alright. You don't have to be nervous."

"I'd like for you to hear my confession."

Tuck felt a bit wary of the Englishman in his presence. He might be a spy. He might also be a poor, miserable sinner no different than everybody else in this fallen world. Besides, his job as a priest required him to be as impartial as possible.

"Come into the confessional."

Priest and penitent went into the small confessional located at the back of the church. Vance breathed as he prepared to tell the veteran priest what was on his mind.

"Bless me Father, for I have sinned. It's been a couple of months since my last confession and I accuse myself of the following sins."

There was a slight pause.

"Go on."

"Father, I feel as though I am guilty of an unpardonable sin."

"Oh?" Tuck asked. "Please elaborate."

"I've been dealing with a severe crisis of conscience. As you're probably well aware, I am a member of the Paras. I'm from the midlands of England."

"Just out of curiosity, I know that after the Protestant Reformation, and I'm partly of British descent myself, England went predominantly Anglican. Has your family always been Roman Catholic?"

"Yes it has. Now, they did suffer during specific periods of history, most notably the reigns of Edward the Sixth, Elizabeth the First and under the theocracy of Oliver Cromwell. Anyway, as I was trying to say, I can no longer stomach having to witness atrocities carried out not only by the North American government, but my own as well. I don't know what to do, Father. I'm nearing the point of desertion."

"I believe the unpardonable sin you're referring to is high treason," Tuck stated. "This is a very complicated manner. You, like countless young men in generations past, enlisted in your country's armed forces mainly out of a sense of patriotism. Am I correct?"

"Yes. But as I said, I just can't take any more of this."

"Son, if you don't mind me asking, what is your name?"

"Brian Vance. I'm twenty-one years old. Joined the Royal Army after graduating from high school."

"You're probably not married."

"I have a fiancé back in England. I'm dying to see her again."

"Brian, you have not committed any sins by not wanting to partake in the genocide that is occurring all around us. Come into my office for a minute."

Tuck and Vance exited the confessional. The church was empty at this time in the afternoon. Vance followed Tuck into his office. Tuck pulled a business card from the pocket of his clerical shirt.

"Any time you wish to talk to me, call the church and we will arrange a time. But whatever you do, be extremely discreet about it." Tuck had a strange gut feeling that this embattled young soldier could be of help to the resistance, but he wasn't about to jump to any wild conclusions just yet.

"Thank you, Father Tuck." Vance placed the card in his pants pocket. "We'll talk soon."

Chapter 57

Given the dire circumstances in which they found themselves in, life was slowly returning to normal for Jake, Mallory and Kevin. A blistering hot summer was giving way to a crisp, cold fall. With most of their food stores depleted, the three remaining members of the resistance group spent much of their days hunting and preserving meat for the incoming winter.

Under a slate-gray, cold late September sky, Jake smoked pieces of venison from a recently killed deer. Of late, the rebel leader had noticed that the cold was affecting his joints. He seemed too young and fit to be getting arthritis. This was the last thing he needed right now. Jake turned around as Mallory exited the small entrance to the abandoned mine carrying two steaming mugs of tea. She handed one to Jake. They sipped slowly, letting the hot beverage warm their insides.

"Thought you might enjoy this." Mallory wrapped her hands around the hot mug. She could sense the sadness and hopelessness coming from within him. "I completely understand how you feel, Jake. I wish I could say something that would make it all better."

"She's the only woman I ever loved. Sure, I'd had my share of relationships before, but Nicole is everything I've ever wanted in a life partner."

"Jake, each day I pray that Nicole and Arielle are alive and well."

Jake set his tea on the small table next to the rack where the venison was smoking. Unable to hold it back any longer, he broke down crying. Mallory set her tea down as well.

She hugged him tightly.

"Jake, it's going to be alright. I know how badly you desire to be reunited with them, how you want to get back into the city and exact retribution against every one of those evil people. And I truly believe that if it is God's will, we will find a way to do just that."

*****

Although the district government had implemented a severe crackdown on almost all forms of dissent in the city, that crackdown was beginning to backfire. Each day, under the watchful eye of NAP forces as well as the contingent of Norwegian peacekeepers who'd arrived recently from Kamloops, residents took to the streets in large demonstrations. Food had become scarcer and, with winter just around the corner, the populace was in full-out panic mode. Frank Carragher was beginning to wonder if his little empire was starting to crumble. If it did, his future working for the North American government was gone.

Robert Hunt and the small group of rebels knew that this increase in civil upheaval was an opportune time to carry out another attack. It was a moonlit though chilly night. Hunt, Marty Smith, Jeff Hinton, Ben Hinton, Father Tuck and Chris Templeton gathered in the furnished basement of Hunt's home. Over the past week or so, Tuck had been meeting secretly with Brian Vance. He enjoyed talking with the troubled young British paratrooper and believed that he could be swayed to the other side. At the same time, Tuck was still not one hundred percent sure that he could trust Vance. He dared not mention their meetings with his fellow insurgents.

As well, the veteran priest had been spending some time getting to know Sarah Jane Pierce. Although quite antireligious, Sarah Jane nonetheless enjoyed having somebody to talk to. As far as she was concerned, Tuck was not working for the authorities and most likely despised them as much as she did.

"It is time to carry out another attack," Hunt stated rather bluntly. He looked over at Chris Templeton. "Chris, you've been doing a bit of scouting around lately. What have you found?"

"Couple of the downtown restaurants, you know, the upscale ones, they're often frequented by NAP personnel as well as Norwegian and British troops. There's one particular scumbag who's a regular at the Café Monaco down in Sixth Avenue."

"Yeah, who's that?" Smith asked.

"Jean-Pierre Bisseau. To the best of my knowledge, he's originally from Montreal. That piece of shit is complicit in the murders of at least fifteen city residents," Templeton explained.

"What are you talking about, Chris?" Hinton asked.

"This isn't a well-known fact, but on the day of the occupation, in addition to those who were deemed subversive and locked up either in the regional jail or sent to labor camps, a handful were simply executed. A couple of those individuals were Peter Rollins and Jack Hemphill," Templeton explained.

"Peter Rollins?!" Smith was aghast in horror. "Ole Pete ran one of the largest gun shops in Kamloops for years!"

"I've heard," Templeton said as he continued talking. "As I was about to say, they were all taken to the old landfill on the south end of town and shot."

"Dad." Benjamin looked at his father with great concern in his eyes. "We must avenge their deaths."

"Don't you worry son. We're doing just that."

"He often goes there with his family. Bisseau has two young daughters. I believe the family lives in the West End," Templeton stated.

Benjamin's eyes lit up excitedly.

"I say we target his family as well. The only way that we are going to win is by striking fear deep into the hearts of every one of those bastards."

"No, we can't do that," Hunt stated. "We never want to lower ourselves to their level."

"So how do you want to go about doing this?" Smith asked.

Templeton stood.

"The old Irish Republican Army used to employ a tactic that effectively struck fear into the enemy as well as their loved ones," he explained. "Years ago, during the period known as the 'Troubles' in Northern Ireland, Provisional IRA cells would target members of the Royal Ulster Constabulary as well as guards that worked at Long Kesh Prison in Belfast. To use an example, a target would be eating at a local restaurant. An IRA member, his face concealed by a ski mask, would assassinate the mark in front of his wife and children."

"That does sound a little brutal but doing so would definitely send a message that we are not fucking around," Hunt said. "I don't know about the rest of you guys, but it certainly sounds like a plan to me."

Chapter 58

Jean-Pierre Bisseau raised the porcelain cup to his lips. He sipped slowly, savoring every drop of the strong-tasting expresso, one of the two dozen or so signature coffees on the menu at Café Monaco. Bisseau, a native of Outremont, a Montreal suburb, had spent nearly twenty years as a member of the Sûreté du Québec. A year earlier, he joined the North American Police with the rank of captain. Bisseau, his wife Sophie, and their daughters, Madeline and Josee, sipped hot drinks as they waited for their meals to arrive.

The popular downtown Kamloops eating establishment was quite busy every day around lunchtime. Bisseau felt somewhat like an outcast. Patrons looked upon his black uniform with scorn and contempt and avoided him as much as possible. The veteran police officer realized that he was taking an enormous risk bringing his family to the other end of what used to be the nation of Canada. With the recent killings of his colleagues, he too feared that his own life could be in danger as well as the lives of his wife and children.

A cool breeze blew down Sixth Avenue. Chris Templeton stood against the west-facing outer brick wall of the small plaza that included Café Monaco. Slightly nervous, he touched the handle of the .45 ACP which was tucked discreetly inside of his jacket. Templeton stole a brief look inside of the packed eatery. Bisseau, his wife and daughters were sitting in the middle of the restaurant eating sandwiches and salads. Templeton donned a black balaclava and went inside.

The next few seconds seemed like forever; everything went into slow motion. The former Canadian soldier received curious as well as frightened looks from patrons and staff. His heart beating wildly, Templeton made a beeline for Bisseau. Madeline gasped in horror as a man wearing a mask and brandishing a pistol with a sound suppressor on the end of it approached.

"Daddy!"

As Bisseau went to turn, Templeton shot him in the head. The NAP officer fell off of his chair onto the floor. Templeton fled out the backdoor of Café Monaco into an alleyway. Not one of the patrons got up from their seats to assist. A devastated Sophie fell to her knees. Mother and daughter cried in unimaginable anguish. One older man got up from his table and flashed a taciturn glance at the grieving widow before leaving the restaurant.

Templeton double-timed it down a narrow alleyway. He'd already ditched the .45 in a sewer hole. He ran right to Fifth Avenue where Jeff and Ben Hinton waited with nervous apprehension inside of a Honda Civic outside of the King Cinemas. Templeton spotted the car. He sprinted over and jumped in the backseat.

"You got it done?" Jeff asked.

"That piece of rubbish will never harm another human soul." Templeton was breathing heavily. "Let's just get the hell out of here."

*****

Nicole did her best to relax on top of the covers of the queen-sized bed in Frank Carragher's bedroom. An old movie played on the big-screen perched on the wall directly in front of the bed. Although Nicole felt as though she was going against everything she stood for by working for the enemy, it at least kept her sane. Arielle was enrolled in Grade Two in an inner-city school, now under the mandate of the federal Department of Education.

Nicole continued to feel somewhat disconnected from Arielle. She wondered if it was too late to save her only child. Only time would tell. It had been several weeks since Nicole had spoken with Father Tuck. She was also quite concerned about Bridgette. Although Nicole desperately wanted to speak with Tuck, any contact with the renegade priest whatsoever would likely raise suspicions. Nicole had officially become Frank Carragher's prized possession and he watched her like a hawk.

Arielle was in her room playing Wii. Carragher was in the washroom adjacent to the master bedroom running a bath. Recently, the manipulative star bureaucrat had been placing immense pressure on Nicole to have sexual relations with him. She brushed off his advances but knew that she could not do so forever. Carragher emerged from the spacious washroom with nary a tack of clothing on him. Nicole recoiled at the sight of the pasty white skin, that burgeoning mountain of fat that nearly buried his midsection, and hairy chest and stomach.

"My dear." Carragher failed in his attempt to speak in a sexy, seductive tone. "Would you be so kind as to join me? My back and shoulders are just killing me this evening."

There was no way that Nicole was getting out of this one and she knew it. Slowly, the attractive woman arose from the bed. Next, she slipped off her nightgown.

Carragher became aroused at the sight of her slim, toned figure.

"You and I are going to have a lot of fun together."

Nicole felt nauseated as she followed Carragher into the bathroom. The whirlpool-style tub was filled with hot water and bubbles. Carragher got in. She followed suit.

"Now pleasure me like I've never been pleasured before," Carragher instructed as he relaxed in the hot water.

Chapter 59

The aggressive campaign to root out and destroy Jake Scribner and the remaining rebels intensified into the fall. The NAP strike teams were joined by units from the Norwegian Special Forces. Recently, the occupying forces had located the group's former base camp in the midst of the Bonaparte Plateau. The ramshackle cabin was exactly where Sarah Jane had told them it was. Upon blasting the cabin and adjacent buildings back to the Stone Age, crews sifted through the remains for bodies. To their chagrin, there was no evidence whatsoever of anybody even being there.

"I knew that little bitch was lying to us!" Major Toombs' face was crimson-red as he stood in Frank Carragher's office. "She was merely buying herself more time. Sir, we must torture her until she tells us exactly where Jake Scribner, Kevin Sorenson and Mallory Hutchinson are hiding."

"Major, perhaps you didn't check the remains thoroughly enough. Bodies would be charred, almost impossible to identify. Guerrilla bands have a tendency to be very mobile."

"I spent the better part of twenty years chasing after guerrillas. I know everything there is to know about them."

"Well Major, if you think it will do you any good, by all means, be my guest. I meant to ask you, what is your opinion of that Norwegian colonel?"

"He's a good soldier. Believes in what he's doing."

At that moment, Nicole entered the office. She was dressed professionally in a knee-length skirt and blazer.

"Mr. Carragher, I have all of those reports typed up. Would you like me to mail them directly to Denver?"

"If you don't mind I'd like to give them all a once-over first. Just set them on my desk."

"Not a problem at all," Nicole said before leaving the office.

Toombs continued to be displeased with his supervisor's decision to bring Nicole Clare into their lives.

"Sir, with all due respect, I cannot understand for the life of me why you are foolishly trusting that woman with confidential information. Considering the fact that she was once engaged to Jake Scribner, she has only one intention and that's to destroy us. Whatever you do, Sir, don't let your guard down. You'll regret it."

"Major, I have enough shit on my plate at the moment and don't need you treating me like an errant child. Ms. Clare is a changed woman. Call me old-fashioned, but I still believe in giving people a second chance."

Chapter 60

Father Tuck had been especially cautious in his approach to arranging this secret meeting. As the veteran priest got to know Private Brian Vance, it became clear that the young Brit was not only going to desert his post, he was on the verge of switching sides. Tuck had made it known at a meeting a few nights earlier that a deserter was about to join their ranks. Right off, Jeff and Benjamin Hinton as well as Marty Smith accused Tuck of collaborating with the enemy. The young, hotheaded Ben Hinton had even threatened to shoot Father Tuck right there in Robert Hunt's basement. Tuck had braced himself for this reaction by his compatriots.

Once Hunt had heard the very compelling reasons as to why Brian Vance was crossing the floor, he reluctantly convinced the others to meet with him. Hunt, Smith, Templeton and the Hintons sat around the small room located at the back of Sacred Heart Church anxiously awaiting their meeting with Brian Vance who was, for all intents and purposes, still the enemy. The doorknob slowly turned. Father Tuck entered with a fresh-faced youth with a crewcut. Hunt and the others rose from their seats. It was plainly obvious that Vance was as nervous as they were.

"Brian," Tuck said. "I would like to introduce you to Robert Hunt, Marty Smith, Jeff Hinton, Ben Hinton and Chris Templeton. Bob is the leader of our little group. He's a retired RCMP officer."

Hunt and Vance shook hands.

"Nice to meet you Brian."

Vance shook hands with the other members.

"I guess we should get started then," Tuck said.

Everyone sat around on the old couches and chairs.

"So Brian, Father Tuck explained to us why you have deserted," Hunt stated.

"I just believe that this entire occupation is illegal. The world conflict taking place right now was completely engineered by the world's banking elite and the military industrial complex. Secondly, I'm British. I have many ancestors who moved to Canada. As well, I have relatives living here now, mainly in Victoria and Vancouver. I can't do this. I mean, suppress people who've done nothing to me."

"I understand fully," Hunt stated. "My grandfather served with the Twelfth Manitoba Dragoons during the Second World War. I myself gave this country over thirty years of service."

"Mr. Hunt," Vance asked. "What are your plans to take back the city?"

"As of right now, nothing," Hunt replied with a slight chuckle. "It's just a miracle that we haven't gotten caught yet. I have to admit Brian, we were all hesitant to meet with you at first. But since I've spoken to you in person, it isn't hard to see that you're the genuine article. I'm just glad that the citizens of Kamloops have the cajones to fight back. Those protests are growing by the day. It's a sure sign that the occupiers are losing ground. I'm sure you've heard about Jake Scribner."

"I certainly have. He's the modern-day Robin Hood who's been wreaking havoc in this district for months." Vance stated.

"I don't know Scribner that well, but his fiancé's parents, God rest their souls, were good friends with Barbara and I. We knew them mainly through church. Father Tuck, have you had any contact with Nicole Clare since she was sent to live with Carragher? I just hope she doesn't betray us."

"Nicole is our greatest asset," Tuck said. "When the moment is right, she will take down that power-mad murderer herself. No, unfortunately I haven't. Hopefully one of these days though I will."

Chapter 61

Nicole had to prove her loyalty to the man who considered himself her 'benefactor'. Frank Carragher did his utmost to convince Nicole that she could do nothing without him. How deluded he was. It was a crisp Saturday afternoon. Nicole opted to spend the day by herself shopping with the generous sum of Ameros Carragher had given to her. Arielle was attending a party for the children of federal government officials and NAP officers posted in Kamloops.

It was nearing three o'clock. Nicole was required to contact Frank Carragher's office by dinnertime and report to a designated location where she would be picked up. The leaves of the maple trees along the downtown street where she walked were bright orange, red and yellow. All of a sudden, Nicole remembered where she was; directly across the street was Sacred Heart Church. Although she desperately wanted to go inside, the strong possibility that Carragher had some of his minions trailing her made her hesitant. She'd carried that feeling of suspicion and paranoia around with her all day. Nicole had not spoken with Father Tuck in weeks. She was concerned that her impromptu visit could jeopardize both their lives.

Nicole entered. It was peacefully quiet inside. A trio of older ladies she didn't recognize sat near the front reciting the rosary. On Saturday evenings, mass was held at five. Confessions generally began two hours prior. Not that many people-especially those of her generation-bothered going to confession anymore.

At that moment, a man exited the confessional. Nicole drew a deep breath to calm her body before going in. She kneeled down. Father Tuck's face was obscured by the customary screen.

"Bless me, Father, for I have sinned. It's been years since I made my last confession. I haven't exactly been an angel if you know what I mean."

"You and I both," Tuck replied.

"This is Father Tuck, is it not?"

"Yes," Tuck answered a bit guardedly. "Do I know you?"

"It's me. Nicole Clare," she responded in almost a whisper.

Before Tuck even had a chance to respond Nicole had the screen pushed over.

"Nicole!" Though excited, Tuck kept his voice to a minimum. "How are you? How'd you manage to...?"

"I don't have much time to talk."

"Are you and Arielle okay?"

"We're hanging in there. You don't have to worry. I've got that demented piece of garbage wrapped around my little finger and he's too dumb to see it. I must have inherited my mother's charm."

"What are they getting you to do?"

"Mainly typing up documents. Press releases and whatnot."

"And Arielle? She's alright?"

"To be quite honest with you, Father, I fear it might be too late."

"Too late?"

"They've brainwashed the poor kid. Molded my sweet little girl into a cold, mechanical shell of her former self. Deep down, I know that she still loves me. I just think about all of those children who were stolen from their parents. Do you believe that they can be reprogrammed?

"Only God knows that."

"I'm constantly thinking about Jake. I can't live knowing that he's gone forever."

"You know Jake better than you know yourself. He's very much alive."

"Don't be so sure."

"I'm quite sure," Tuck stated. "Close to a month ago, there was an ambush that resulted in the deaths of two members of Jake's group. A young woman who fought with them was captured."

Nicole felt a renewal of hope inside of her.

"Who is that?"

"Her name is Sarah Jane. She's Bridgette's cellmate."

"So you don't know where Jake is?"

"If I knew that, they would have killed me by now. Sarah Jane flat-out refuses to tell them. Anyway, you'd best be getting along. You can be rest assured that the pieces of our plan are slowly being put into place."

Chapter 62

The thumping of boots across the hard concrete floor indicated to Sarah Jane that something very bad was about to happen to her. She and Bridgette had been sitting in their cell talking when, at the sound of a buzzer, the door opened. Paynter and two officers, one of which was Stanford, stood outside.

"Pearce. Come. Get moving." Paynter ordered.

Sarah Jane was escorted down a corridor toward the janitorial room where she'd almost been drowned a couple of weeks earlier. Her entire body became weak and she trembled. Toombs and Gardiner stood outside of the small interrogation room. Her legs buckled with fear. Sarah Jane was forcefully placed onto a chair. She cowered as Paynter and Toombs loomed over her.

"Ms. Pearce." Toombs spoke with a thick Alabama accent. "It would appear that you intentionally provided us with false and misleading information. Perhaps you are not aware, but such an offense carries twenty years of hard labor minimum."

Sarah Jane's heart beat fiercely. Just as she had feared, it would only be a matter of time before they discovered she'd lied to save her friends.

"We bombed that cabin you told us about north of Porcupine Meadows Provincial Park," Paynter stated. "Checked all through the remains. Not a trace of Jake Scribner, Kevin Sorenson or Mallory Hutchinson. You're playing with fire here. I seriously advise that you stop jerking us around."

Paynter's face contorted in rage as she got within inches of Sarah Jane's face.

"Where are they you little bitch?!" She slapped Sarah Jane hard across the face. "If you refuse to tell us, we are going to do unspeakable things to you."

Stanford and another officer, a young man named James, looked on as Gardiner grabbed Sarah Jane roughly and flung her against cement brick wall. She crumpled to the floor cringing in agonizing pain.

"Captain, I'd say some good old-fashioned electric torture is in order here," Toombs said.

"I couldn't agree more," Paynter replied. "Sergeant Gardiner, get the machine ready."

In one corner of the room was a machine with wires and clamps connected to it. While Gardiner got the electronic torturing device powered on, Stanford and James bound Sarah Jane's wrists. They proceeded to tie the terrified young woman to a ceiling beam when Father Tuck entered the room.

"What in the name of God is going on here?!" Tuck was aghast.

"This is none of your concern, Padre," Toombs snapped. "I politely request that you get the hell out of here."

Tuck was not backing down.

"You have no right to do this. The mistreatment of prisoners is condemned under the Geneva Convention."

"You really think I give a rat's ass about some document the North American government has not ratified and will never?"

"The priest is right," Stanford stated.

Paynter and Toombs glared upon the young correctional officer with daggers in their eyes.

"How dare you speak in such a way?!" Paynter laid right into her subordinate. "I could have you arrested for sedition. You wouldn't like that, would you, Officer Stanford?"

"I'm just stating a fact ma'am. I took law courses in university. And we are still bound by international law."

Tuck stepped forward.

"Please, for the love of God, allow me to talk to her-alone."

Paynter and Toombs cringed at the idea.

"If you honestly believe that you are going to talk the information out of her, Padre, you're even dumber than I thought," Toombs said. "Gardiner, turn that machine off. I guess it's only fair that we give Miss Pearce here a little more time to think about what she is going to tell us."

Toombs, Paynter, Stanford and James exited the room. Sarah Jane sighed in relief as Tuck unbound her wrists.

"If you hadn't have come, I'd probably be half-dead by now." Sarah Jane said.

Tuck leaned in closer.

"Sarah Jane, very quietly, almost in a whisper, I need you to tell me exactly where Jake, Kevin and Mallory are."

Although Sarah Jane trusted Tuck, she still wasn't one hundred percent sure that he wasn't in with the authorities. At the same time, if Tuck intended to head up there to bring her friends back to Kamloops to finish the fight, she should tell him. Looking around to see if anyone was watching, Sarah Jane put her mouth to Tuck's ear.

"The old Calstar Mine a mile off of the highway just south of Well's Gray Provincial Park."

"Thank you so much. Now I better be getting out of here."

Chapter 63

Frank Carragher knew deep down that he was losing his ironclad grip on the reins of power. Each day, demonstrations against the occupying forces got larger at well as bolder. A couple of days earlier, during a clash with NAP riot squad members, one Kamloops resident was shot and killed. The district administrator wanted to believe that the citizenry didn't have access to anything more lethal than rocks, baseball bats and some Molotov cocktails. But the reality was significantly different.

Although it appeared from the outset that the band of terrorists who'd launched a half-hearted guerrilla campaign for months were finally defeated, another resistance cell had cropped up in the city. Carragher had been shaken by the murder of Jean-Pierre Bisseau. What was even more shocking was the fact that the killing took place in broad daylight in front of dozens of citizens. The fact that none of them cooperated with authorities was hard proof that they no longer had any support from the populace. The North American Police and United Nations forces under his command had control of the city for the time being, but if the way things were eroding was any indication, that control would be wrested away.

Toombs entered his superior's office.

"Good morning, Sir."

"Good morning, major. Any leads in your investigation of the murder of Captain Bisseau?"

"Unfortunately not, Sir. Mr. Carragher, you recently had a meeting with Senator Grimshaw. I remember Grimshaw years ago when he was a city councilman in Birmingham."

"Yes, he's a remarkable fellow indeed. As true a southerner as can be found. Well, not as true as you, major, but pretty darn close."

"I admire the compliment, Sir."

"Have you spoken with Lieutenant-Colonel Mullen lately? I was hoping to touch base with him. Every time I call over to the command centre, he's busy."

"Mullen is doing well. He's been having to deal with a disciplinary issue with one of his men."

"Oh?"

"Some young fella skipping duty, getting a little too friendly with the locals."

"That's always cause for concern. I trust that Mullen will get this nipped in the bud before it spirals out of control."

*****

Father Tuck prayed discerningly about the decision he was about to make. The veteran pastor asked God to guide him through the endless security points as well as the probing drones and helicopters that patrolled the skies. Robert Hunt and the members of his small resistance cell were elated that Tuck was going to go into the mountains, track down Jake, Mallory and Kevin, and bring the remaining three rebels back into the city.

Once the three were back in town, all of them, including Brian Vance, would hold one more clandestine meeting to hammer out a strategy to drive the North American and United Nations forces from their district once and for all.

Tuck had filled a backpack full of provisions. The naturally-inclined athlete laced up his hiking boots and threw on a warm jacket. After locking up the parish house, Tuck drove through Kamloops in his jeep until he reached the Red Bridge that spanned the South Thompson River. Three British paratroopers were guarding it. Tuck rolled down the driver's side window.

'Good day, Father," a young lance-corporal said. "Where are you off to today?"

"I'm visiting a colleague of mine who lives in 100 Mile House. Father Hebert."

"May I see your travel permit please?"

"Why certainly."

Tuck fished out a forged travel permit and handed it to the British soldier. The para looked it over and handed it back to Tuck.

"Here you are, Father. According to the conditions outlined in this permit, you'll be gone for four days."

"That is correct."

"Carry on then."

Tuck put up his window and drove north onto Mt. Paul Way. An enormous sense of relief washed over him. Tuck pulled onto Yellowhead Highway 5 and continued driving north.

The once picturesque countryside had been permanently scarred by the horrors of war. Houses previously owned by wealthy local businesspeople and ranchers sat abandoned. Others had been destroyed in air attacks. Tuck drove for over an hour. He spotted the faded sign signalling that the tiny hamlet of Little Fort was coming up.

As Tuck drove past Little Fort on the Trans-Canada Highway, he noticed that the once touristy community was nearly empty. A few locals wandered the main street. Tuck's destination was Clearwater. Prior to reaching the mountain town, he pulled off of the Trans-Canada and made his way down a barely-used bush road.

Tuck parked the jeep in a section of secluded forest that was very thick. He locked the jeep, opened up the back hatch and retrieved the backpack. It was a sunny though bitterly cold day. Tuck zipped up his jacket and covered his head with a woollen toque. He stared into the vast wilderness that was laid out in front of him. He had a rough idea where the mine was located. Tuck had hiked this area a few times before. It was rocky, treacherous terrain, but he could handle it.

Chapter 64

Jake warmed his hands over the small open fire that had been constructed near the mouth of the abandoned mine. The trio had spent a good portion of the day chopping and splitting firewood. Kevin tinkered with the radio. It had recently stopped working. Mallory, feeling a bit antsy, went outside for a walk. It was late afternoon. She breathed in the cool, fresh air. A shudder shot through Mallory's body as she heard a sudden noise. Her eyes darted in all directions. The young woman froze as a tall man dressed in warm clothing, his eyes obscured by sunglasses, suddenly emerged from the forest. Mallory quickly retreated inside the mine.

"There's somebody out there!"

Kevin set his tools down. Jake stood up.

"Just one person?" Jake asked. If indeed a Special Forces team had snuck up on the encampment, they would all be in the process of being killed right now.

"Yeah." Mallory breathed heavily. "I couldn't get a good look at his face."

Jake reached for the AR-15 leaning against a wall.

"Kevin, grab one of those rifles. If this individual is hostile, he won't be getting any closer than he is right now."

Jake and Kevin stepped outside. They raised their weapons at eye level at the stranger in their midst. He acted as though he already knew them.

"It's okay. I'm from…"

"Do not proceed any further," Kevin ordered. "This will be your first and only warning."

"Please identify yourself," Jake commanded.

Tuck removed the toque and sunglasses. Jake was shocked to see a familiar face standing no more than twenty meters away from him.

"Father Julian Tuck? I'm so sorry. If I had have known…"

"Don't worry about it," Tuck said.

"How did, I meant to say, how were you able to get up here?"

"I did something no man of the cloth is supposed to do," Tuck replied with a wry smile. "I had to employ some good old-fashioned bullshit."

"You're in good company," Kevin laughed.

Jake and Kevin lowered their rifles. Jake pumped Tuck's hand.

"It's great to see you again, Father." Upon seeing Tuck, the lingering question that had been burning inside of him for the past six months automatically returned. "What happened to Nicole? I just remember that horrific day back in April. Oh God, I hope she isn't gone permanently."

"Nicole is alive and well. So is Arielle."

Jake's eyes went as wide as saucers.

"Where are they?"

Tuck followed Kevin and Jake into the living area of the mine. Tuck removed his coat, which Mallory hung on a wall hook.

"On the same day that you fled into the mountains, they were arrested and detained in the former provincial jail," Tuck explained. "It's currently being used as a 're-education' camp. Anyway, about a month ago, Nicole and Arielle were sent to live with Frank Carragher."

"Who is Frank Carragher?" Jake asked.

"The administrator of the Thompson-Nicola district. Guy is a power-mad control freak. He has a predilection for using woman as his sex slaves."

"Thanks for the heads-up, Father," Jake said. "I'm dying to wrap my hands around his throat."

"Father…? Sorry, I don't know your name," Mallory said.

"Julian Tuck. I'm rector of Sacred Heart Parish in Kamloops."

"Our friend was captured during a battle over a month ago," Mallory explained.

"Her name is Sarah Jane Pearce," Tuck said.

"You know her?!" Mallory's eyes went wide with excitement.

"I've talked to her a few times. She's being held at re-education centre."

"How is she doing? I doubt they'd be treating her very hospitably."

"They aren't. They've been coercing and even torturing Sarah Jane into telling them the location of your hideout."

"That would explain all of those helicopters and jets flying around here blowing up everything that remotely looks like an enemy base," Jake said. "So, how did you find us?"

"I've been counselling Sarah Jane," Tuck replied. "Two nights ago, after I saved her from a round of electric torture, she very discreetly told me. Jake, the biggest reason I risked my life driving up here is to bring you all back to town. It's time to finish this fight once and for all."

Jake was a bit taken aback.

"Father, realistically, there is no way that the three of us can merely sneak back into Kamloops, kill a thousand or so NAP and UN soldiers, rescue Nicole and Arielle-it isn't like I haven't dreamed of doing such a thing-and then liberate the entire city."

"What do you think I've been trying to tell you since we got into this mess?" Kevin said to Jake with a laugh.

"Perhaps you're all not up on current events, but an active resistance movement is growing within the city. There are riots every day. Believe me, we are winning. There have been bombings, assassinations of NAP officers, sabotage. People are sick and tired of being treated like slaves and they are not going to take it anymore," Tuck said.

"Getting back to Nicole," Jake said. "Where is she and Arielle living now? I know for a fact that Nicole would never do such a thing willingly."

"Carragher has a mansion in the West End. But he spends a good portion of his time in the seat of power for the entire district, which is the Canfield Building downtown."

"The resistance in the city. How much are you privy to it?" Kevin asked.

"I'm actively involved. I'm their eyes and ears inside of the detention centre. Jake, do you know a gentleman by the man of Robert Hunt?"

"Name doesn't ring a bell. Should I know him?"

"Bob and his wife are, or should I say were good friends with Nicole's parents. They were killed, in case you didn't know. Anyway, Bob is a retired RCMP officer who lives in the city."

"We also have another unlikely ally in this fight. There is a young British paratrooper who's been secretly working with our group. He's going to get us onto the base," Tuck explained.

"The base?" Mallory asked.

"Yeah, the old Kamloops Airport. It's the official nerve centre for the North American Police and United Nations forces that are in charge of policing the district. Rumors are swirling around that there is going to be a massive riot tomorrow evening. That will keep the majority of the troops tied up. As soon as we get in, there's a meeting at Hunt's house. If everything goes as planned, it will finally be over tomorrow evening."

Chapter 65

Nicole continued to find herself in an incredibly vexing quandary. Agreeing to become Frank Carragher's chattel had been the only way she could have escaped indefinite detention. The more Nicole came to the realization that this heartless ruler had strong feelings for her, and merely wasn't using her as his plaything, it sickened her stomach. A few nights earlier, facing the threat of banishment to a labor camp and Arielle being sent to a state-run boarding school in Arizona, Nicole reluctantly pushed herself to have sexual relations with Carragher. Afterward, she felt violated. At this point, the future for both her and Arielle was looking bleak.

When not working at the district headquarters, Nicole was usually confined to Carragher's mansion endlessly cooking, cleaning and scrubbing it. It was exhausting, tiring work. She had just taken a roast chicken out of the oven when Carragher walked in. Arielle had gotten home from school an hour earlier. She sat at the kitchen table doing her homework.

"That smells delightful, dear. You must have slaved over a hot stove for hours."

"More than you'll ever know," Nicole replied with a hint of cynicism in her voice.

Carragher sat down at the kitchen table.

"Nicole, I've been thinking. Since it appears that you and I are going to be together forever, we soon should start having the 'discussion.'"

Nicole shuddered inside. No way in hell was she ever going to marry this freak.

"I'd love for you to become my wife. You satisfy me in a way no woman ever has before."

'Perhaps that's because I'm being coerced into doing so you fat, controlling pig', Nicole thought to herself.

"It's quite obvious how much Arielle enjoys being here," Carragher continued. "She and I have been getting along very well. Nicole, if you've learned one thing about me it's that I always get what I want. I'm not asking for your hand in marriage-I'm demanding it. Failure to accept this generous offer will not bode well for you and her."

Frank Carragher simply could not help but be a manipulative, conniving son-of-a-bitch. She would like nothing more than to rip off his balls. The situation was going from bad to worse and there was nothing that she could do about it.

"Frank, I'm really going to have to give your proposal some consideration." Nicole acted as though she might take him up on it. "Don't get me wrong. I immensely enjoy being in your company…"

"Really?" There was a sudden change in the tone of his voice. "Perhaps it's just me being overly paranoid, but I find that hard to believe. Last night, you seemed to find my body repulsive. That's going to have to change really fast if we are to be husband and wife. Remember, Nicole, you are not indispensable. There are dozens of other women in this city who would eat shards of glass to be where you are right now. You really have to start proving your loyalty to me and stop beating around the bush."

Even in pressing moments such as this, Nicole knew how to play the game. She removed her oven mitts and put her arms around Carragher. Although it sickened her to do so, she started kissing him passionately.

"Is that what you were looking for?" she asked in a seductive tone.

"You read my mind."

Chapter 66

Father Tuck spent the previous night with Jake, Kevin and Mallory. The rebels had ditched the jeep in the mountains. In its place they procured an old truck from an abandoned property outside of Clearwater. Jake, Mallory and Kevin huddled in the back of the truck, the bottom of which was covered by straw. It was an old Ford, built sometime in the early 1980s. Kevin assumed it had been used to haul swine.

The truck vibrated as Tuck drove into the outskirts of Kamloops. He slowed down as he approached the bridge that crossed the South Thompson River that connected Highway 5 with Battle Street. Four British paratroopers guarded the bridge. A sergeant, a slightly plump older chap with scattered wrinkles in his face and silver hair, motioned for Tuck to stop.

"Good evening," the sergeant said as Tuck manually rolled down the driver's side window. "Your travel permit, please."

Tuck displayed the phony document.

"Where're ya coming from, Father?"

"100 Mile House. Visiting a colleague of mine up there."

"Don't you normally drive a jeep?"

"Drove the same vehicle for ten years. It was some reliable. She just creamed on me last night. Didn't give me any warning either. Engine's gone. It will be cheaper just to get a new vehicle than fix this one. A local farmer sold this old beater to me."

The sergeant peered over at his younger subordinates.

"Check the back."

Jake felt his heart sink into his stomach at the sound of footsteps approaching the back of the truck. His right hand clutched a Beretta. There were five rounds in the magazine. A young private opened up the flap, unaware that three rebels were stowed away underneath of it. He was nearly knocked flat on his feet by the stench.

"Oh, I failed to inform you," Tuck said. "The farmer used this truck to haul pigs. I'm terribly sorry."

The sergeant shook his head angrily.

"Ah, the hell with it. Alright, Father, you may pass."

Jake, Mallory and Kevin felt a tremendous surge of relief as the truck proceeded into Kamloops. All of them were itching to finally see an end to the brutal occupation and seek retribution against all of those responsible for violating their rights. Justice would be served but at the end of a gun. Mallory was elated knowing that her best friend had survived. Kevin continued to bellow in shock at having to witness his nephew being blown to bits in front of his very eyes.

*****

It was promising to be another potentially lethal day. As thousands of city residents poured through Seymour Street, a large force of Norwegian soldiers and NAP troopers were waiting to put an abrupt stop to them.

The riot control squads had been issued full body armor, shields, helmets, batons, tear gas, guns that fired rubber bullets as well as water cannons and riot shotguns. NAP sharpshooters were posted on the roof of the Canfield Building as well as some other government offices. Extra members of the British Parachute Regiment were deployed to guard bridges, leaving only a skeleton crew to keep watch over Kamloops Airport.

While NAP and British operators were overwhelmed communicating with crews on the ground, Toombs, Mullen, Karlsen, Wynne and Brown gathered inside of Mullen's office.

"I just spoke with Carragher," Toombs stated. "He wants to have a few Apaches on standby."

"I was really hoping that it wouldn't turn into a bloodbath," Karlsen said. "Unfortunately, I don't see any way in which we can avoid that. I spoke with General Nilsson. Edmonton is awash with civil strife as well," the veteran Norwegian Army officer explained. "It will be hard to get reinforcements for at least a day or two."

"We're not going to need any reinforcements," Toombs said with confidence. "If I have my way, every one of those animals will be mowed down."

"Major Toombs, that isn't really necessary," Karlsen said.

"Then what is necessary, Colonel? Do you think we should be coddling them? No more fucking around. The gloves are coming off." Toombs turned to Mullen. "Colonel. That soldier of yours. Did he turn up yet?"

"I'm afraid not."

"Sounds quite insubordinate if you ask me," Toombs said.

"Private Vance is a decent soldier. He's just a bit unruly at times. Personally, I don't believe that the kid is cut out for military life, at least not the life of a para."

"I'll tell you one thing though," Wynne said with anger in his voice. "When that little shit does show up again, he better have a damn good explanation. Because if he doesn't, he's going to be court martialed."

"He definitely will be," Mullen stated. "I will personally make his life a living Hell."

Chapter 67

A phalanx of North American Police troopers served as a human barricade against the wild mob that was moving straight for the Jim Canfield Building. Two NAP Mine Resistant Armored Patrol vehicles (MRAPs) were parked in front of the district headquarters. Two troopers sat in the turrets of the armored fighting vehicles behind .50 calibre machineguns.

For Major Toombs, the ride from the airport to downtown Kamloops had been a nerve-jangling one. As the APC he rode in made its way down a street adjacent to Seymour, it was pelted by rocks and petrol bombs. Toombs felt unnerved at the sheer number of rioters. Each and every one of them was thirsty for the blood of anybody wearing a uniform. For the first time in his life, he actually felt scared.

A gunner sitting in the heavily-armored turret of the APC fired a few warning shots which echoed noisily in the early evening air. The gunner swivelled around just as two rioters rushed toward the APC. They were armed with wine bottles filled with flammable liquid and with flaming rags stuck in their necks. The gunner unleashed a barrage of .50 calibre cartridges into the rioters, turning them into flying chunks of flesh.

The APC drove further down the street. The driver pulled into the fortified parking lot behind the Canfield building. Hundreds of rioters were drawn to the chain-link fence that protected the parking lot. Several of them attempted to climb the fence but were repelled by the razor-sharp concertina wire atop it.

The back of the APC flew open. Toombs got out very quickly, as did the gunner, the driver and two other NAP officers.

Half a dozen NAP troopers stood guard inside the foyer of the Canfield Building. Toombs got inside the elevator and went up to the eighth floor. Carragher was in his office eating a late dinner with Nicole and Arielle.

"Major." Carragher rose. "If our troops cannot keep back those unruly hordes, I will order you to use lethal force."

"Sir, my Apache crews are on standby. It's unfortunate that the British Army helicopter crews had to be sent down to the border. We could really use them tonight."

"We work with that we have," Carragher stated. "Anyway, Major, I would really like to spend some quality time with my future wife and stepdaughter. I know that you will go above and beyond your scope of duty to keep us all safe."

Toombs half-saluted his boss.

"You don't have to worry about that, Sir. You're in good hands."

*****

The nerves of the staff at the re-education centre were frayed as a massive mob moved toward the facility. Paynter ordered each of the one hundred and twelve officers in the facility to don full riot gear. The secured armory was opened up. Officers armed themselves with shotguns, .45 APC handguns and C8 carbines. Officers posted inside of the five guard towers that ringed the perimeter of the prison were ordered to shoot any demonstrators that got within ten meters of the fence. The entire facility was placed in lockdown. This was much to the chagrin of the inmates.

Sarah Jane, Bridgette and twenty fellow female prisoners inside of their unit held their ground defiantly as Paynter and ten officers entered. They were wearing bulletproof vests, helmets with visors and carried shields and batons.

"You are all to return to your cells immediately," Paynter said.

There were shouts of 'no' and 'fuck you bitch' as the inmates began shouting and yelling at the officers. It didn't bother Paynter one bit. The inmates, including Bridgette and Sarah Jane, got right in the faces of their warders.

Paynter nodded at her officers, who violently herded the boisterous inmates back into their cells. They got hit and kicked hard in the shins in the process. As Bridgette and Sarah Jane were being forced back into their cell, Bridgette looked at Stanford, who was sitting in the pod. He appeared upset, as though he wasn't comfortable being there.

Once all of the prisoners were back in their cells, Paynter and the officers left the unit. Paynter knocked on the door of the pod. Stanford opened it.

"Officer Stanford, you're in charge of watching over each of the cellblocks. There could be potentially thousands of hooligans making their way to the facility tonight. I expect we'll be getting assistance from the NAP and possibly the UN. We'll need helicopters to disperse the crowds. But in the meantime, we're in total lockdown. Nothing gets in or out. Understand?"

"I understand perfectly, Captain."

"Good."

Paynter left.

Chapter 68

Jake, Kevin and Mallory showered and changed their clothing at the home of a Kamloops resident who was sympathetic to the resistance. After all those months of living in the wilderness, a hot shower and shave felt pretty good to Jake. Tonight, considering that he was going to be reunited with his long lost love, he needed to look his best. Afterward, the three rebels and Father Tuck drove over to Robert Hunt's house. Barbara had made coffee and sandwiches for everyone.

There was an applause amongst the group as Jake, Kevin and Mallory descended into the basement.

"So this is the legendary Jake Scribner," Benjamin Hinton said.

"You know what they say. Legends never die," Jake rejoined with a smile. "Guess that means I'm going to live forever."

Robert Hunt held out his hand. Jake shook it.

"It's great to finally meet you, Jake."

"The feeling is mutual, Robert." Jake pointed at Kevin and Mallory. "These are my counterparts Kevin Sorenson and Mallory Hutchinson. We have more than enough stories to tell about our time in the mountains."

Kevin and Mallory shook hands with Hunt.

"I'll introduce you to the members of my little resistance group. Jake, these fine, upstanding ruffians are Marty Smith, Jeff Hinton, his son Ben, and Chris Templeton. Like yourself, Chris is also a veteran."

"You were in the Canadian Army?" Jake asked Templeton.

"Special Operations Group. I hear you were a combat controller in the United States Air Force."

"My original plan was to become a fighter pilot. God didn't bless me with twenty-twenty vision so I had to settle for calling in fighter jets to bomb enemy positions. Don't worry. It was every bit as thrilling."

Hunt patted Brian Vance on the shoulder like a proud father.

"This young man here is going to be our ticket onto that base," Hunt stated. "The same base we are going to completely destroy."

"You're that British paratrooper," Jake stated. "The one who switched sides."

Vance nodded.

"What made you want to help us out?" Jake asked.

"I have my reasons. Biggest one being that I can no longer stomach the sight of my fellow countrymen committing war crimes. I realize that I can no longer return to England. That's a sacrifice I'm willing to make. Probably be spending the rest of my life here."

"Let's get this meeting started," Tuck said.

The rebels took their seats. Barbara brought down a tray holding a steaming coffee pot, sandwiches, cups and saucers.

"This is the plan that we've devised," Hunt stated. "Taking back our city requires a three-pronged strategy. First, we seize control of the airport. There will be a skeleton crew on duty there tonight, so, providing Murphy's Law doesn't sneak its way in and fuck up our plans, we should be able to do it."

The rebels starting pouring cups of coffee and eating sandwiches.

"As well, we will destroy the main communications centre and kill all UN soldiers and NAP officers we encounter." Hunt looked over at Marty Smith, who was enjoying a roast beef sandwich. "Marty, you up for flying into the belly of the beast?"

The former Canadian Forces helicopter pilot continued to fly search-and-rescue missions for a civilian company that serviced much of northern British Columbia.

"You better believe it," Smith replied.

"The next stage of our assault," Hunt continued. "Will be seizing control of the Canfield Building. Most of the UN and NAP forces will be focused on quelling the riots so getting in there shouldn't be the most difficult task in the world though it will be far from easy. The third and final stage, and I have no idea how this will go down, is taking back the provincial correctional centre and rescuing all of the political prisoners inside."

"Robert," Smith asked, "You've been telling us that you have a man on the inside at the jail. Can you finally divulge his name?"

"Ryan Stanford."

Jake was feeling quite restless. Although these plans sounded fireproof, he knew from firsthand experience that things could go south in a hurry. A lot of moving parts in orchestrated union.

"Robert," Jake asked. "Do you think Nicole will be at the Canfield Building?"

"Most certainly," Hunt replied. "Carragher, regardless of how many guards he has, would be reckless to stay in his home with all of those ticked off city residents roaming around. He'd most likely find his head on a pike. Don't worry Jake. You and Nicole will be together once more." Hunt looked over at Templeton. "Chris, we'll need you to put your sniping skills to good use. There's a building directly across the street from the Canfield. Metrolife Financial. I need somebody to go with you. I'm not sure who though."

Mallory raised her hand. "I'll go."

All eyes looked upon the normally reserved young woman with surprise.

"Ms. Hutchinson, this is an extremely volatile situation," Hunt said.

"What do you think I've been doing for the past six months? Painting my nails?"

"You don't have to take my word for it," Jake said proudly. "But Mallory is an excellent shot. She has taken out her share of enemy troops."

"I learnt from the best," Mallory said with a wink as she look at Jake.

Templeton turned to Mallory.

"Alright then kiddo, you're coming with me," Templeton stated.

Chapter 69

Brian Vance tried to forget how uneasy he truly was going back into the base. He sat behind the wheel of a British Army truck the rebels had stolen earlier. Vance drove up to the gate of the base. Jake, Father Tuck, Jeff and Ben Hinton, Robert Hunt, Marty Smith and Kevin Sorenson were in the back under cover grasping a variety of automatic firearms.

Pete Huggins had just reached the halfway point of a detective novel he picked up a week earlier. As the truck drove up to his window, Huggins was shocked to see who was driving it.

"Brian? Where the hell have you been mate?! Wynne is going to have your hide."

"Don't worry. I checked in with Lieutenant Brown several hours ago. He assigned me to deliver some supplies to the bridge crews," Vance explained.

"That's a relief. We all figured you went AWOL. Anyway, pass through. Enjoy the rest of your evening."

Vance drove into the expansive compound. Other than two fellow paras who were patrolling the parking lot and tarmac on foot, it was devoid of human life. Vance drove around the terminal into a parking lot. He got out of the truck and opened up the back flap. Benjamin Hinton, his hair cut short and face shaven, wore British Army fatigues. He was disguised as a para.

"Follow me guys," Vance said.

The group went inside of the terminal. Right in front of them was an elevator.

Vance turned to Jake and Kevin.

"They're going to shit when they see what we've brought in," Vance said with a smile.

"It's the last thing any of them will ever do before we send them off to the afterlife," Jake replied.

Jake and Kevin held their hands out in front of them. Benjamin placed handcuffs around the wrists of both men.

The insurgents went into the elevator. It took a minute to reach the fourth floor of the former airport terminal. Vance and Ben were brandishing L85A5 assault rifles with silencers on the ends of them. The elevator door opened with a pinging sound. They slowly stepped out into a corridor. The entire building was eerily quiet.

"Father Tuck," Vance stated. "I'm going to get you, Marty, Jeff and Robert just to lay low in that office for the time being. We'll come back and get you once we get this out of the way."

The four men walked to an office located along the corridor. Vance and Benjamin escorted their 'prisoners' down the corridor until they reached the communications room. Vance knocked on the door. A British Army corporal named Hodges, whom Vance barely knew, opened it. Five other operators-three of them NAP troopers-and two from the British Army-sat at their workstations.

"You're not authorized to be in here," Hodges said sternly to Vance and Ben Hinton. "Where did these prisoners come from?"

"We caught them not too far from here," Vance explained. "Buggers were armed too. We couldn't take them to the detention centre."

One of the NAP operators, a young woman in her mid-twenties, was shocked when she recognized Jake Scribner.

"Hey, that one looks like..."

"That's because it is," Jake replied with a devious smile.

As the operators reached for their side arms, Vance and Ben unleashed a torrent of lead into them. In less than a minute, all of them lay dead amongst high-tech computer systems that were flaming and smoking from having been shot up. Ben quickly removed the handcuffs from Jake and Kevin. The amped-up rebels retreated into the corridor. Jake knocked on the office door. Hunt answered it.

"Now onto phase two," Jake said.

*****

Mullen, Wynne and Karlsen sat around the officers' lounge located on the fourth floor. Wynne listened as though he had heard something. He sniffed at the air.

"Smoke." He got up from his chair. "My God, there's a fire!"

At that moment, Vance, Kevin, Jake, Ben and Jeff, Hunt and Smith burst inside the lounge. The military officers reached for the 9mm handguns on their belt holsters but were quickly thwarted by the better-armed rebels.

Mullen was beside himself.

"Vance, what's the meaning of this?"

Vance pointed his rifle at the colonel's face.

"Colonel Mullen, you are about to pay for the crimes you've committed against humanity. There's a reason I didn't shoot at those people you ordered slaughtered."

"You son-of-a-bitch!" Mullen lashed back. "You took an oath to Her Majesty the Queen. To your country. You're going to face the death penalty for high treason."

*****

The smoke from the shot-up communications centre was seeping into the corridor as well as through the roof of the building. Pete Huggins had left his post for a minute to stretch his legs. He spotted the smoke. Huggins quickly went back into the guardhouse and pressed the button signifying a red alert. Within seconds, a piercingly loud buzzer went off.

Inside the officers' lounge, the rebels and their captives listened at the loud, incessant buzzing sound.

"Appears the only way you'll be leaving here is in a cadaver bag," Wynne said evilly.

Jake looked around at his compatriots.

"I say we waste every one of them right now."

"I second the motion," Jeff Hinton said.

Mullen, Wynne, Brown and Karlsen looked on in paralyzing fear as the rebels aimed their rifles at them.

"Come on, Brian!" Mullen was breathing hard, begging for his life. "I promise, you will not be punished."

"Colonel, I know better than to believe such a lie from you. If you have any last words, say them now. That goes for all of you."

Twelve base personnel, a mixture of British and NAP members, raced up a flight of stairs to the fourth floor of the terminal. Pete Huggins was in the lead. All of a sudden, they heard the sound of screams followed by gunshots. Huggins' heart raced wildly. He sensed something very bad was happening.

The group moved quickly down the corridor. Without warning, Jake, Robert Hunt and Vance appeared from the officers' lounge. They opened fire on the base personnel. Two British soldiers and an NAP trooper fell dead onto the concrete floor. A fierce firefight ensued as both sides ducked in and out of doorways all along the corridor exchanging gunfire.

Ben Hinton had difficulty concentrating amongst the rush of violence which the youth was unfamiliar with. All of a sudden a bullet struck his upper arm. He fell back into the officers' lounge. Jeff rushed to help his son.

Hunt barely missed getting hit in the chest. He ducked into a room and swung back out, shooting Huggins directly between the eyes. Vance felt terrible for seeing his close friend dead but this was not the time for sadness. As the battle continued, Kevin Sorenson appeared from behind a door. The bear of a man handled an L7A2 machinegun as if it were a toy. He unleashed a merciless torrent of 7.62x51mm cartridges into the remaining enemy soldiers and police, mowing each of them down.

Jeff Hinton rifled through the lounge, eventually finding a first aid kit. He began wrapping dressing around Ben's wound. Although bloody, the bullet had passed through.

"Oh God, it hurts!" Ben yelped in pain.

"I know it does, son. We're getting it taken care of."

While Hinton and Tuck tended to Ben, the others walked down the corridor. Kevin kept the machinegun pointed as he moved forward. At the end of the corridor was a middle-aged man with a moustache. He wore the flight suit of an NAP pilot. The man, who didn't appear to be hit, was traumatized and barely able to move.

"Please. Don't kill me." The pilot pleaded in a thick Missouri accent. "I have a wife and three kids back in Joplin."

"You should have thought about that before coming up here," Jake said.

"We better waste him," Vance said.

"Wait a minute!" Smith intervened. "He could prove useful to us. This man is a helicopter pilot."

Jake turned to him.

"We already have one pilot on this crew. Yourself."

"I've been thinking about something. Each of the bridges around the city is heavily guarded by paras. We're going to have to take them all out," Smith said.

"So what's your plan, Marty?" Hunt asked.

"I've flown different aircraft in my lifetime. Figure I can fly one of those Apaches sitting out there on the tarmac."

"I don't think that's a very wise idea," Jake said. "You've never flown one of them before."

"I know a lot about those types of helicopters," Smith explained. "If I can learn on the fly, on pun intended, you can use him to pilot one of the Bells and bring all of you into the city." Smith turned to the pilot on the floor. "What's your name?"

"Bill…Bill Hochner."

Jake and Kevin grabbed Hochner and brought him to his feet.

"Alright Bill, you're going to be flying my colleagues and I into the city," Jake stated. "And if you try anything funny, it will not bode well for you. Do you understand?"

Hochner nodded. Jake looked over at Smith.

"I really hope you know what you're doing."

"Relax, would you? It will be like learning how to ride a bike."

Chapter 70

Upon securing the airport, the rebels had cut the fuel lines on all of the helicopters, save for three, an Apache, a Blackhawk and a

Bell Huey. It took Marty Smith about fifteen minutes or so to figure out all of the controls of the Apache. A bit nervous, the experienced pilot started up the attack helicopter and flew off into the night air.

Robert Hunt kept a pistol trained on Hochner's head as the captured NAP pilot started up the gears of the Bell Huey. Once everyone was inside, Jake lit a match and dropped it into the highly flammable gas that was seeping all over the pavement. Then he ran toward the Bell Huey. As Hochner was taking off, the entire fleet of patrol and attack helicopters erupted in a succession of loud, fiery explosions.

*****

Major Toombs peered through the window at the end of the corridor on the seventh floor of the Canfield Building. Far below, NAP troopers and Norwegian peacekeepers were in a vicious clash with the ever-growing mob of furious Kamloops residents. Toombs' heart felt heavy. They were safe, but for how long? Frank Carragher rushed out of his office.

"Major, I just got off the phone with General Meers in Vancouver. We can forget about reinforcements arriving any time soon. The airport has been destroyed."

"Goddammit." Toombs stewed angrily. Deep in his heart, he knew Jake Scribner was very much alive. "Any response from Mullen or Karlsen?"

"I'm afraid not," Carragher answered.

Nicole and Arielle sat restlessly in Carragher's office. Nicole held Arielle in her arms. Lately, she'd begun to notice the child coming around, slowly warming up to her again. Perhaps the months of brainwashing were coming undone. The joy Nicole felt about her beloved hometown finally being liberated was almost overwhelming. As much as he had his delusions, Frank Carragher would never have Nicole Clare as his own.

*****

It had been relatively easy for Chris Templeton and Mallory Hutchinson to gain access to the eight-storey Metrolife Financial building in downtown Kamloops. She grasped a captured British Army sniper rifle while her comrade-in-arms held onto two MBT LAW antitank weapons. As was expected, the entire building was deserted. Since the elevator was out of service, they had to climb eight flights of stairs to reach the roof.

Down below on Seymour Street, the violent clashes continued. A NAP sharpshooter positioned on top of the Canfield Building fired, striking down a demonstrator who charged at a line of riot police with a machete. All of a sudden, over one thousand rioters removed glass liquor bottles and flammable liquids such as lamp oil and turpentine from their bags and began constructing Molotov cocktails.

Five minutes later, the wall of NAP troopers and Norwegian peacekeepers found themselves assailed by a storm of flaming bottles. They were forced back as the Molotov cocktails erupted into bright orange fireballs as they smashed into the pavement or against their hard plastic shields. The smell of noxious fumes permeated the air.

Toombs watched from the window. He spoke into a radio. "Strike down every one of them," he ordered.

The machine gunners atop the MRAPs fired off a volley of .50 calibre bullets that tore into the heavy mass of humanity. The crowd retreated in a panicked state as their colleagues lay dead or severally injured on the blood-soaked pavement. Body parts were strewn everywhere.

Chris Templeton and Mallory Hutchinson were slightly winded by the time they reached the roof. Wasting no time, Templeton flipped up the LAW's sight. He focused it on one of the APCs. A missile swooshed through the air and hit the turret dead-on. The armored fighting vehicle exploded, resulting in a flaming, burning hulk of steel. Like a bolt right out of blue, a bullet flew out of nowhere, narrowly missing them.

Templeton and Mallory quickly ducked. Mallory peered through the sight of the sniper rifle. She caught a glimpse of a NAP sniper embedded amongst the heaters and pipes of the Canfield Building roof. She breathed as she placed the crosshairs on the masked man's underbody, took aim and fired. He fell over onto his back, dead. Templeton raised the other LAW. Quickly, he arose from his hiding place and fired a missile into the second APC. The rocket struck the heavily-armored vehicle underneath. A massive explosion ensued, knocking the APC over onto its side.

*****

From where Marty Smith sat in the somewhat uncomfortable cockpit of the Apache attack helicopter, the entire city appeared as though it was an enormous soundstage for the big-budget Hollywood production of a post-apocalyptic blockbuster film. The night was dark and cold. There were fires everywhere. Smith steadied the chopper's controls as he flew in the direction of the bridge the traversed the South Thompson River where Fortune Drive connected with Victoria Street.

Smith used his helmet-mounted display, the Integrated Helmet and Display Sighting, to aim the M230 30mm chain gun exactly where he wanted it. Five British paratroopers standing on the bridge appeared to take little notice of the Apache helicopter flying in their direction. All of a sudden, they were assailed by a punishing volley of 7.62 rounds from the 30mm cannon, which cut all of them down. Smith continued flying in an easterly direction. He was bound and determined to take out each of the bridge checkpoints.

*****

Hochner's nerves were frayed to the max as he flew the North American Police Bell Huey helicopter into the warzone that had become downtown Kamloops. Robert Hunt, sitting in the cockpit next to Hochner, kept the pistol levelled at his head. In the back, Jeff Hinton sat with his son. Ben's wound had at least stopped bleeding. Tuck sat amongst them. Kevin manned the chopper's M240 heavy machinegun. Jake had a cable attached to the belt around his waist. The plan was for Hunt to lower Jake onto the roof of the Canfield Building-that is, if they weren't all killed in the process.

"Are you ready, Jake?" Hunt asked.

Jake was psyching himself up to make his move.

"As I'll ever be."

From inside of Carragher's office, the district administrator and Major Toombs watched as the helicopter hovered in the night sky a few feet from the roof.

"Thank the maker we're getting out of here in one piece," Toombs said contentedly.

Four NAP snipers perched on the roof of the Canfield Building watched as Hochner lowered the Bell Huey. One of them, a corporal named Dobson, thought it somewhat peculiar that one of his colleagues would be manning the M240 dressed in civilian attire. Dobson flinched as he heard Toombs' voice come through the radio on his helmet.

"Dobson, get your men to stand down. We're being evacuated. I'm sending a team up to the roof. Mr. Carragher, myself, his fiancé and her daughter are coming up next."

"Roger that, Sir," Dobson replied.

Lieutenant Dwight Hawkins, a long-serving member of the Arkansas State Police who'd joined the North American Police not long after its inception, ran through the hallway with the NAP troopers. They ascended the stairs to the penthouse and ran out onto the roof.

Dobson and the three other snipers were waiting as Hawkins reached them. Suddenly, Kevin unleashed a hail of 7.62x51mm cartridges into the nine NAP members. Hunt turned around.

"You gotta go now, Jake."

Jake hung on tightly to the cable. Controlling the wench, Father Tuck lowered him slowly onto the roof. It was something the former Special Operations soldier hadn't done in years and he was quite nervous.

Chapter 71

Each of the correctional officers posted on high alert inside of the re-education facility understood that they were about to be embroiled in the fight of their lives. A crowd numbering in excess of five thousand city residents, many walking, just as many driving, was making its way down the Trans-Canada Highway directly for the former provincial jail. The handful of officers posted on the facility's guard towers had frayed nerves as the crowd mobbed around the fence surrounding the sprawling complex.

Most were armed with a plethora of homemade weapons including crudely-built explosives though quite a few had firearms. The officer standing on the tower beside the outer entrance aimed his C8 carbine and fired at a group of demonstrators who had begun to climb the fence. He knew though that it would be folly to believe that he could hold them off forever.

From nowhere came an Apache attack helicopter. Its rotor blades sliced through the air like razor-sharp cutting knives. Many in the crowd began to panic and flee as the monstrous flying death machine flew overhead.

By now, Marty Smith had gotten the hang of flying the Apache. He fired the M230 chain gun, reducing the guard tower next to the entrance to a shell of metal and glass. The burgeoning crowd cheered voraciously when they saw that the chopper was on their side. Smith zipped around the east-facing perimeter of the prison. A correctional officer standing on the east tower shot at the incoming Apache with his carbine. A couple of the bullets reflected off of the chopper's tough outer shell.

Smith hit a button that controlled the gunship's missile pods. In seconds, a Hellfire missile flew out and slammed into the tower, blowing it to smithereens.

*****

Jake had hit the ground running as soon as he landed on top of the roof. The ex-combat controller peered over the side of the building. By now, the mob was in the process of overwhelming the NAP and UN personnel on Seymour Street. Jake fled for cover at the sound of the penthouse door opening. Toombs rushed out onto the roof accompanied by two NAP troopers. He glared upon his slain colleagues with horror.

Inside the Canfield Building, Frank Carragher ushered Nicole and Arielle into his office. He then locked the door behind them. Carragher opened one of the drawers in his desk and produced a Browning 9mm, the one he'd been issued by the Department of Justice for personal protection.

"Can't you see what's happening?" Nicole had pleasure beaming in her eyes. "Jake has returned to seek revenge against you and your occupying hordes. You actually believed that I cared about you? I was just stringing you along the entire time."

Furious from all of the activity taking place around him, Carragher pushed Nicole against a wall. She struggled as he held his considerably heftier frame against her small body. He put the Browning to her head.

"You continue to have delusions of grandeur about your knight in shining armor coming to save you! You're mine. Bought and paid for. And you will marry me whether you want to or not."

Arielle pushed at Carragher and tried to get him off of her mother.

"Leave my mother alone you big freak!"

Carragher pushed the little girl aside. He focused his attention back to Nicole, his eyes filled with rage.

"To ensure you don't decide to flee, I'm confining you to this office. And on the off chance that your Romeo decides to waltz in here and rescue you, I'm going to have a bit of insurance, so to speak. Your brat stays with me."

"You touch her I swear to God I'll rip your head off!" Nicole was seething in fury.

Carragher laughed mockingly at her.

*****

Jake hid behind a large ventilation system. He took deep, controlled breaths. His heart beat wildly as the two NAP troopers moved in his direction. His sweaty right hand gripped a Beretta pistol. At that moment, Jake leaped up from behind the ventilation box and shot the two of them. Toombs reacted by firing several shots in Jake's direction. Jake ducked for cover as two rounds hit the ventilation box.

"Is that you hiding behind there, Scribner?" Toombs advanced forward, a .45 aimed directly at the ventilation box. "I knew all along that you'd come back for that mouthy wench of yours."

Jake jumped up from behind his hiding place and fired a shot that narrowly missed his adversary. The senior NAP officer returned fire. It was hard to see in the darkness.

"You're a little too late. Nicole belongs to somebody else. She wouldn't want you anymore anyway."

Jake couldn't contain his anger any longer. He sprung on top of the ventilation system and kicked Toombs in the head. The NAP major went down. The .45 went flying.

"I'm going to make you sorry you ever heard of me," Jake said with fire in his eyes.

Jake raised the Beretta. To his chagrin, it was empty. Smiling devilishly, Toombs quickly got to his feet. He unsheathed the combat knife hanging from his duty belt. Toombs charged at Jake, who missed the knife by inches. Toombs unleashed a relentless, vicious attack, stabbing and slashing at the rebel leader, who did his best to deflect and parry the thrusts.

"Hey Scribner, ever hear of the expression 'death by a thousand cuts' cause that's exactly how you're going to die."

"Ever hear of the expression, 'don't bring a knife to a gunfight?'"

Toombs looked at him strangely. Jake suddenly dropped to the ground, rolled over and grabbed Toombs' .45. Jake fired three shots; one in the chest, one in the stomach and to finish, one in the head.

Jake stood over Toombs' dead body.

"You can't say I didn't warn you."

Chapter 72

Janet Paynter steeled her nerves as the infuriated masses of Kamloops residents burst through the gate of the facility and gathered inside of the main parking area. They were out for blood. It would only be a matter of time before they breached the main secured entrance. Bridgette and Sarah Jane looked anxiously through the bars of their cell, as did all of the other inmates in the cellblock. Every officer in the facility had assembled in the main foyer that served as a connecting point for the other areas of the prison. Stanford watched anxiously as his fellow guards got ready to make their stand.

Outside in the parking lot, the crowd parted ways as a man driving a bulldozer drove up to the main entrance and began ramming the piece of heavy machinery through it. The legion of heavily-armed correctional officers stood almost shoulder-to-shoulder in the main foyer. They raised their weapons as thousands of townsfolk poured into the prison through the administration area like a swarm of deadly hornets.

"Hold steady!" Paynter commanded.

The mob stormed down a corridor toward the foyer.

"Fire!"

The thick phalanx of correctional officers fired a devastating volley into the mob. Several went down but the rest made a beeline for the officers. In seconds, the outnumbered prison guards found themselves engaged in a gory, fierce hand-to-hand battle.

Ryan Stanford had been waiting for the exact moment to do his part for the resistance. During the past few months, he had had a couple of discreet meetings with Bob Hunt. Stanford had been working at the jail when the occupation began but, like Brian Vance, could not abide actively taking part in the violation of citizens' rights. He pressed the buttons that opened each of the cells in every cellblock.

Paynter looked on in horror as the inmates massed into the foyer and joined their fellow citizens in beating and stabbing the officers to death. Terrified for her life, Paynter went to run but was blocked by Bridgette and Sarah Jane.

"Karma's a bitch, isn't it, Paynter?" Sarah Jane said.

Paynter, who grasped a shotgun in her trembling hands, shakily pointed it at the two inmates but they wrestled it away from her.

Although she could have never envisioned herself doing such a thing, Sarah Jane knew in her heart that this cruel, cold-hearted bitch needed to die. She aimed the shotgun right at Paynter's head. Paynter was so scared that she could hardly speak.

"This is for all the hell you put everybody through," Sarah Jane stated before she pulled the trigger. Paynter's head exploded in a blast that caused blood and brains to fly in all directions.

"You know," Bridgette said. "The Bible does say that one shalt not kill. I've had many a fellow Christian say that covers everything. As far as I'm concerned, it's wrong to commit murder of innocent people. It isn't wrong though to destroy the evildoers amongst us."

"Bridgette, I'm an atheist as well as a pacifist and even I can agree with you on that one," Sarah Jane replied.

*****

For several minutes, Jake had been trying to find his way around the Canfield Building. He had no idea where Nicole was and the proverbial clock was ticking. All of a sudden he heard the faint sound of yelling and banging. It was coming from the eighth floor. Jake darted up a flight of stairs. Far below was a large open area where the building's swanky lobby was. As Jake rounded a corner, Frank Carragher appeared from out of nowhere. He grabbed the back of Arielle's jacket with one hand and pointed the Browning 9mm at Jake with the other. Arielle trembled with terror at Carragher, then pointed the pistol at her head.

"So you're the legendary Jake Scribner? The man who singlehandedly destroyed my domain. You turned an entire city of people I so desperately wanted to serve against me."

"Carragher, the only person you've ever wanted to serve is yourself."

"Jake, help me!" Arielle pleaded.

"You may have won this round Scribner, but you will never get to hold the most precious jewel in your life ever again…or her sweet little girl!"

Arielle struggled against Carragher's grip. She bit down hard on his hand. Carragher yowled in pain. He let go of the child. As Arielle ran towards Jake, Carragher raised the revolver. Jake whipped out his Beretta and fired, hitting the district administrator in the chest. Injured, Carragher kept coming at Jake. Jake slammed Carragher in the stomach area with a sidekick. He doubled over writhing in pain.

"Oh come on. Is that all you've got?" Jake taunted him.

Carragher got back up. He lunged at Jake, who grabbed the overweight man and, using a judo-style throw, tossed him over a railing to the lobby far below. Carragher was impaled on the tip of a flagpole that held the national flag of the Republic of North America.

"How's that for poetic justice you fat piece of garbage?"

Jake coughed up a spitball that landed right on Carragher.

Nicole banged on the locked officer door.

"Jake! Jake!"

Jake and Arielle rushed down the corridor to Carragher's office.

"Nicole, move out of the way. I'm going to kick the door in."

Nicole moved to the back of the office. With one solid front kick, Jake booted in the door. He wasn't inside the office ten seconds before the long-separated lovers fell into each other's arms.

"You probably already knew this," Jake said. "But it was beyond lonely out there in the mountains without your body beside mine. We will never be apart like this again. That I can promise you."

"Deep down, I knew you would not only survive this awful ordeal, but would use your elite military skills to restore freedom to our beautiful little part of the world."

Chapter 73

It was a happy ending to a long, arduous ordeal. Once the residents of Kamloops had taken back the former provincial correctional centre, all of the child detainees were reunited with their loved ones. Jake, Nicole and Arielle received a thunderous applause from the massive crowd that had packed into Seymour Street. On a sidewalk, a large group of men armed with rifles and shotguns guarded one hundred or so captured NAP troopers and Norwegian peacekeepers. Among them was Lieutenant Hochner. The bodies of hundreds of NAP troopers, UN soldiers and townspeople who'd been involved in the rebellion were strewn wildly across Seymour and adjacent streets.

Kevin Sorenson, Marty Smith, Jeff and Ben Hinton, Sarah Jane Pearce, Robert Hunt, Brian Vance and Father Tuck waited at the front of the cheering crowd.

Hunt pumped Jake's hand.

"You're the most famous person in this city since I don't know when," Hunt said exuberantly.

"Ironically, neither of us is even from around here."

Chris Templeton and Mallory Hutchinson exited the Metrolife Financial building. They waded through the crowd until they reached their friends.

"Mallory!" Sarah Jane was so overwhelmed by joy. She cried happily.

The girls hugged each other tightly.

After the provincial jail was liberated, Ryan Stanfield changed out of his uniform and joined the others. Stanfield helped Bridgette to locate her son. Nicole spotted Bridgette in the crowd with Josiah and Stanfield. She rushed over to her.

"Bridgette! You're alive."

The two women embraced warmly.

"If I didn't have you to lean on in there…" Bridgette could barely get the words out she was so emotional.

"Is this your son?"

"This is Josiah." Bridgette smiled through her tears. "Josiah, this is Arielle Clare's mommy."

Jake shook hands with several well-wishers before walking over to where Nicole was.

"Bridgette, I'd like to introduce you to my fiancé, Jake Scribner."

"So this is the Jake Scribner everyone's been talking about?" Bridgette said.

"My God, I didn't think that I was this popular." Jake said.

Still very emotional, Bridgette hugged Jake and gave him a peck on the cheek. Jake looked upon Stanfield.

"Are you Ryan Stanfield?"

The young man with broad shoulders and rugged good looks nodded in response.

"It's good to know that there are still some people in this world who will risk life and limb to do what's right," Jake said.

Jake, Nicole, Arielle, Bridgette and Stanfield walked over to where the rest of the group were congregated. Jeff Hinton shook Jake's hand.

"Jake, I don't know what to say but we aced this test." Jeff said with a smile.

"You're like a modern-day William Wallace," Ben stated.

"Well, as far as historical freedom fighters go, I've always been sort of partial to Robin Hood, Spartacus or even Tuvia Bielski," Jake said. "To be honest, I realize that I can take a lot of the credit but certainly not all of it. We did this together." Jake smiled at Brian Vance. "And if it wasn't for this turncoat, we wouldn't have been able to pull off this daring takeover. So Brian, what are your plans for the future?"

"I'm not a hundred percent sure," Vance replied. "I'll never be able to return home. Probably settle somewhere in B.C."

"What will we do with all of those prisoners of war?" Chris Templeton asked. "We can barely feed ourselves right now, much less those pieces of shit."

"They'll be processed, detained, charged with various war crimes," Jake explained. "Some will be locked up while others will get a one-way ticket to the gallows."

"Personally," Kevin said. "If I have anything to do with it, they will all receive harsh punishment. In my opinion, none of them deserve to live."

"I agree with you there, Kevin," Tuck chimed in. "But it is only fair that they receive one final grace from a priest. Even some of history's vilest criminals have confessed during their moment of execution."

Jake put his arms around Nicole and Arielle.

"Whatever happens from here on out, we won't fret about it tonight." Nicole said.

"Where are you going right now, Jake?" Mallory asked.

Jake held Nicole close to him. They kissed passionately.

"Oh, I don't know. Head home. That's if there even is one to go back to. Catch up on some much-needed sleep as well as lovemaking. I think we all need a heavy dose of R&R before the real hard work of rebuilding begins." Jake said.

THE END

The End

58419399R00140

Made in the USA
Columbia, SC
20 May 2019